'You and I ar
risk-takers, J

Then Finn reached out for her, his arms hard around her waist. This time his intention was quite clear: he was going to kiss her.

'Don't, Finn—please don't. You're changing everything and I don't want that.'

'You can't fool me—you don't play it safe any more than I do.'

'There are some risks I choose not to take. Getting involved with you is one of them!'

Dear Reader

Spring is here at last—a time for new beginnings and time, perhaps, finally to start putting all those New Year's resolutions into action! Whatever your plans, don't forget to look out this month for a wonderful selection of romances from the exotic Amazon, Australia, the Americas and enchanting Italy. Our resolution remains, as always, to bring you the best in romance from around the world!

The Editor

Although born in England, **Sandra Field** has lived most of her life in Canada; she says the silence and emptiness of the north speaks to her particularly. While she enjoys travelling, and passing on her sense of a new place, she often chooses to write about the city which is now her home. Sandra says, 'I write out of my experience; I have learned that love with its joys and its pains is all-important. I hope this knowledge enriches my writing, and touches a chord in you, the reader.'

Recent titles by the same author:

WILDFIRE
THE SUN AT MIDNIGHT
THE DATING GAME

UNTOUCHED

BY

SANDRA FIELD

MILLS & BOON

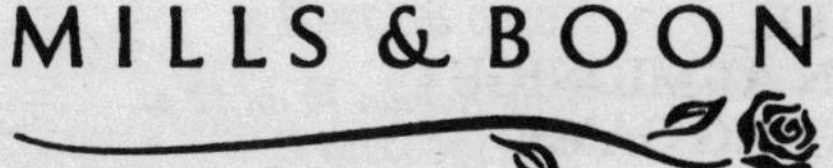

MILLS & BOON LIMITED
ETON HOUSE, 18-24 PARADISE ROAD
RICHMOND, SURREY TW9 1SR

All the characters in this book have no existence outside the imagination of the Author, and have no relation whatsoever to anyone bearing the same name or names. They are not even distantly inspired by any individual known or unknown to the Author, and all the incidents are pure invention.

First published in Great Britain 1995 by Mills & Boon Limited

This edition 1995

ISBN 0 263 78927 6

Set in Times Roman 10 on 12 pt.
01-9504-55764 C

Made and printed in Great Britain

CHAPTER ONE

JENESSA REED swung her four-wheel-drive Toyota into Ryan's driveway and turned off the ignition. What she needed was a hot shower, a home-cooked meal and ten hours of sleep. In that order. Picking up her haversack from the passenger seat, she climbed out of the van and for a moment surveyed Ryan's house with rueful affection.

The architecture, she had long ago decided, could only be labelled Newfoundland Eccentric. The core of the house was square, two-storey and altogether unremarkable, but over the years Ryan had added two porches, a sunroom, a root cellar, a studio where he did folk art that sold like hotcakes to the tourists, and a couple of balconies from which to survey a view that was far from inspiring. Some of these additions had been painted, some not. Two were askew. The overall effect expressed perfectly Ryan's innate exuberance and his total lack of interest in what his neighbours might think.

'I'm home,' Jenessa called, heading for the back porch.

The door opened. 'About time,' Ryan grumbled, taking her haversack and urging her indoors. 'And me with a new job all lined up for you.'

'Oh, no,' Jenessa groaned, 'I've got to recover from the last one first.'

He poured two mugs of ink-black tea from the pot that sat all day long on the stove and said unsympathetically, 'A wild-goose chase makes more sense than tryin' to sight whales in late August.'

She had been guiding a small group of German tourists, who under her tutelage had bagged their limit of Atlantic salmon and had then requested to be shown whales. 'I drove the entire length of the northern peninsula, just about froze to death out on the ocean and was seasick twice.' Jenessa grinned. 'But we saw fin whales, humpbacks and porpoises—so my clients were happy.'

'Hope they tipped good.'

'Enough so I don't need another job right away.'

'You're to meet some guy by the name of Finn Marston tomorrow night on the late flight. Said he'd explain what he wanted when he got here.'

'How long does he want me for?' she said in a resigned voice.

'Didn't say. Forceful kind of guy—didn't give me much chance to get a word in edgeways. Plus it was a lousy connection—he was callin' from some place in Indonesia.'

Anyone who could prevent Ryan from taking his fair share of the conversation had her instant respect. 'Indonesia...did he speak good English?' she asked. She had spent ten days in July trying to teach the intricacies of fly-fishing to three admittedly very handsome but unilingual Spaniards.

'Yeah... he's Canadian, by the sound of him.'

'I wonder why he's coming?' Jenessa said. 'I suppose he wants to catch the last of the fishing season... I'll tell you one thing—he'd better not have ocean-going mammals on his list.'

She levered the lid off the can sitting on the table and helped herself to one of Ryan's molasses cookies. 'You made these because you knew I'd be back today, didn't you?' she added, smiling across at Ryan. He never hugged her when she came home, but he would make sure she had all her favourite things to eat.

'Gotta put some flesh on your bones,' Ryan muttered. He was a small man, no taller than her five feet eight, and wiry as a fox, his beard and hair still showing vestiges of their former fiery red, his eyes a snapping brown. He was her one tie to a life that had fallen apart when she was thirteen; Jenessa valued him both for that and for himself. Father-surrogate and true friend—not a bad combination, and one she knew she was fortunate to have.

Taking another cookie, she said with a caution that in the past had often been justified, 'You did tell this Finn Marston that I'm a woman, right?'

Ryan dunked his cookie in his tea. 'Well, now, not sure I did. Like I said, I didn't get much chance to talk. This guy's more used to givin' orders than listenin' to other people, I'd say.'

'Ryan, I wish you wouldn't do that to me,' Jenessa complained. 'I hate turning up at the airport when someone's expecting a six-foot hunk of brawn in a red flannel shirt and what they get is me instead. All you have to do when you're talking to them is use the correct pronoun—she. One short word and that does it.'

Ryan and she had had this discussion before. 'And lots of them wouldn't hire you then; you know that as well as I do, Jenny. I keeps my mouth shut, they get the best guide this side of Gander airport—and we're all happy.'

Jenessa rolled her eyes. 'You're the best guide this side of anywhere—maybe you should go to the airport to meet the forceful Mr Marston.'

'I taught you everythin' I know and I'm too old to go crashin' around in the woods.' He leered at her. 'More interestin' things to do round home.'

Not all his interests lay in the areas of folk art and home improvements. Another of them was the widowed Mrs McCarthy, whose lemon meringue pie could have graced any restaurant in Toronto. 'How's Grace?' Jenessa said on cue.

'She's fine,' he answered airily. 'Want some more tea?'

Ryan's tea, taken in any quantity, would corrode a moose hide. 'I'm going to clean up,' Jenessa said. 'Any messages for me?'

'Ruth called. She wants you to go over and see the baby after supper. It's got a tooth, she said. Can't see what's so special about that; we all got teeth.'

'It's their first baby, Ryan; of course they think he's special.'

'Not so special I see you makin' any moves to get one.'

Surprised, Jenessa stopped midway across the kitchen. 'What do you mean?'

'You're pushin' twenty-six and I don't see no signs of you gettin' yourself hitched.'

She felt a pang of mingled hurt and dismay. 'Don't you want me living here any more, Ryan?' Her eyes widened. 'Are you and Grace planning to get married?'

'Course not! She'd have me paintin' the balcony and mowin' the grass; she likes things all shipshape, does Grace. And I'm not about to change my ways.' His brow wrinkled in one of the formidable frowns that signified deep thought. 'In the last five years you've met more men than a stag has cows. So how come you haven't married any of 'em?'

She said flippantly, 'None of them asked me.'

'You don't even date 'em!'

'They're my clients, Ryan; there's such a thing as professional ethics.'

Ryan's opinion of professional ethics was both brief and perilously close to obscene. Jenessa added suspiciously, 'Are you sure you don't want Grace to move in here?'

He opened the oven door. 'As sure as I am that if you don't hustle my roast'll be ruined.'

Jenessa left the room, trailing upstairs to her bedroom, whose balcony overlooked a clump of wind-scoured spruce trees. Ryan had never before implied that he even noticed her single state, let alone that he thought she should end it. Maybe—she blinked at herself in the mirror—he wanted to dandle her own baby on his lap. It was the nearest he would get to being a grandfather, after all.

Ryan? Interested in babies? She had to be joking.

Oddly unsettled, she gathered up some clean clothes and headed for the shower. But three hours later, when she was sitting in Ruth and Stevie's kitchen with baby Stephen regarding her unwinkingly from solemn, navy blue eyes, Ryan's remark was still on her mind.

'You look very thoughtful,' Ruth commented.

Ruth's husband Stevie was a wilderness guide, like Jenessa, and Jenessa had met Ruth through him. The two women had liked each other right away, and if Jenessa had a confidante it was the tall, black-haired Ruth, whose practicality was leavened with a lively dash of romanticism. Jenessa tickled Stephen under the chin, trying to get him to reveal the new tooth, and blurted, 'Ryan thinks it's time I got married and had a baby myself.'

'That's natural enough, I suppose. You are nearly twenty-six.'

'I'm not in my coffin yet,' Jenessa retorted. 'Anyway, I'm not like you. I really have no desire to get married—I never have had.'

'You spent a week with Luis, Sanchos and Miguel and didn't even fantasize about weddings?' Ruth had invited the three Spanish fishermen to a lobster boil in her backyard, including Jenessa in the invitation as a matter of course. Now as she folded a towel with a decisive snap she went on, 'They were awfully sweet, Jenessa, you've got to admit that.'

'I liked them. But I didn't want to marry them.' Jenessa managed a smile. 'Individually or collectively.'

'You didn't lust after them—any of them—even the tiniest bit?'

Jenessa shook her head. 'Nope.'

'You could be so pretty if you just paid a bit of attention to yourself,' Ruth mourned.

'When you're guiding a fisherman through a bog, mascara isn't a top priority.'

'You're not in a bog now,' Ruth snorted, giving Jenessa's jeans and T-shirt a disparaging look. 'Your clothes are clean, I'll give you that. But they're not what you'd call sexy. And I'd be willing to bet you cut your hair yourself last time.'

'With my Swiss army knife,' Jenessa admitted. 'I have another client flying in tomorrow, so I won't have time to get it cut before then, either. Anyway, Ruth, when you're stuck in a lodge miles from anywhere with a bunch of men, which I am a fair bit of the time, it doesn't seem appropriate or sensible to go around flaunting your sexuality. A sure way to get in trouble, thank you very much.'

'I don't think you know how to flaunt your sexuality,' Ruth replied vigorously. 'I just wish you'd go to St John's one of these days and spend the day in a beauty salon. You wouldn't even have to go to St John's—Marylou, next door, has just come back from a seminar there, so she knows how to do all kinds of neat new haircuts. Your hair is such a gorgeous colour...you know that cherrywood paddle of yours, how it shines when the sun hits it? That's what your hair's like—and you're the only person I know with green eyes.' Ruth paused, her head to one side. 'Maybe you just haven't met the right man.'

Jenessa didn't think it was that simple. Touched by Ruth's description, she said hesitantly, 'I know I don't fit...I never have, really. All those women's magazines with their advice on make-up and lovers and clothes—I can't relate to them at all. If you want the truth, they scare me to death. I suppose it's got something to do with never knowing my mother and growing up with my dad at Spruce Pond—no other women there. No other people, come to that.'

'I'm not meaning to be critical,' Ruth said hastily. 'I like you just as you are.'

'That's good,' Jenessa said with an impish grin. 'Because I'm likely to stay this way. I'm not at all unhappy as I am, Ruth. I don't know how to flirt, that's true, and I'm not out plaguing some man to marry me—but I really like my life the way it is. I love my job...how could I ever give that up? Marriage and babies kind of crimp your style.'

'They're worth it,' Ruth said placidly. 'Stephen, my duckie, smile at Jenessa.'

Stephen gave a huge yawn, exposing one tiny pearl-white tooth, and let his head plop against Jenessa's shirt. She held him close, liking his baby-powder smell and his warm weight, yet knowing that in a few minutes she could hand him back to his mother without the slightest twinge of regret. She didn't have any impulsion to have a baby of her own. Or to attract the man whom one required in order to produce the baby. But it was one thing to acknowledge to herself that she didn't fit the normal societal expectations of what a woman should be like, and quite another to have both Ryan and Ruth, in one day, suggesting that she should change her ways.

She was fine as she was. Besides, the man wasn't born for whom she would give up her job.

So why should she change?

Jenessa spent the next day washing and ironing the clothes in her backpack and helping Ryan varnish a pine bench for a customer from Massachusetts. She could have used the time to go to Marylou's and get her hair cut, but some unacknowledged streak of stubbornness kept her from doing so.

That evening she presented herself at the airport just as the propellor-driven plane was coasting toward the terminal. The same stubbornness had caused her to dress in stone-washed jeans and a forest-green shirt with a businesslike leather belt around her waist. She knew most of the small crowd of people waiting at the gate; she was chatting to Ruth's mother and father, who were meeting their youngest son, when the first passenger pushed open the door. While she'd been waiting, Jenessa had conjured up a mental image of the forceful Mr Marston: he'd be short—short men, in her experience, were often aggressive—greying, and would light up a very expensive cigar as soon as he entered the terminal.

She had often played this game; her record of success was interestingly high.

Ten people got off the flight from Halifax. The short ones were women, the sole man with grey hair was

Tommy MacPherson from Norris Arm, and the only one smoking was Ruth's youngest brother, a fact that would annoy Ruth considerably: Ruth was a reformed smoker and dead set against cigarettes.

A tall man with a thatch of untidy dark brown hair had halted just inside the doorway, surveying the small crowd with visible impatience. He was wearing a blue wool shirt, a well-worn pair of jeans and leather hiking boots; a haversack was slung over one broad shoulder. The only thing she had got right, Jenessa thought ruefully, was the aggression.

Quickly she walked over to him. 'Mr Marston?' she said with a pleasant smile.

He did not smile back. 'I'm Finn Marston, yes.' His voice was deep, gravelly with tiredness.

'I'm Jenessa Reed,' she said. 'The guide you hired.'

His lashes flickered. 'I'm not in the mood for jokes.'

'Neither am I,' she said crisply, wishing that just for once she could be taken at face value rather than having to justify her existence to her male clients. 'I'm the person Ryan recommended to you.'

'You've got that wrong. Ryan said nothing about a woman—because if he had I wouldn't have hired you.'

'Well, you did hire me,' she said with another pleasant smile, although this one took more effort. 'And I'm very good at my job. Ryan booked a room for you in the best motel in town; I'll take you there now, if you like. Or do you have other luggage?'

He looked her up and down with an insolence that could only be deliberate, from her jagged crop of toffee-colored hair to the shiny toes of her leather loafers. 'If I hired you, I can unhire you,' he said. 'I'll get a cab to the motel—what name does it go by?'

His hair was as badly in need of cutting as her own, she thought inconsequentially; his eyes were a very dark blue, reminding her in colour, if not in expression, of Stephen's. The stubble of beard on his chin was also dark, and there were dark shadows under his eyes. He looked, she thought with a faint stirring of compassion, truly exhausted: it was a long way from Indonesia. 'A cab won't be necessary; I'll take you. Luggage?'

'Miss Reed, I don't think you heard me—you've just been fired.'

'Mr Marston,' she replied with rather overdone patience, 'this is at least the fiftieth time I've played this little scene. Canadians, Americans, Swedes, Spaniards... hunters, fishermen, photographers... they all think I should be a man or they think it's extremely funny that I'm a woman. But I can give you references from every one of them as to my competence. I do agree with you that Ryan should have told you I'm a woman. I disagree that that should make any difference to you whatsoever.' She smiled at him again. 'The luggage carousel's just started up; we shouldn't have long to wait. That's one advantage of these short hops—the stops are brief. Have you flown far today?'

His mouth tightened. 'Too far to get any enjoyment out of playing verbal games. The name of the motel, Miss Reed.'

She jammed her hands in the pockets of her jeans. 'Are you Canadian, Mr Marston?' As he nodded, she went on, 'Then you surely must be aware that in this country you can't fire someone because of his or her sex.'

'So sue me. There's my bag, and I'm sure the cabbie will know the name of the best motel in town—in a place this size there can't be that many to choose from. Goodbye, Miss Reed.'

She said clearly, 'I wish you luck finding a replacement. Ryan tried four other outfitters because he knew I was just coming off a job, and no go with any of them.' With a tinge of malice she added, 'To further enlighten you as to the law, as a non-resident you can't go further into the woods than eight hundred meters from the highway without a guide. Good luck, Mr Marston.'

Her cheeks were pink with temper and her shirt made her irises look very green. Something flared to life in his somber blue eyes and just as quickly was smothered. 'Thank you for your help,' he said sardonically. Turning away from her, he heaved a battered duffle bag off the carousel and strode toward the exit. She watched as he climbed in the back seat of a taxi and drove off; he did not look back.

From behind her Ruth's mother said, 'My, what a handsome man... I do love those big, rough-hewn men, don't you, dearie? Client of yours, Jenessa?'

Ruth's mother Alice, for all her many good points, was the most avid gossip in town, and her question was a blatant appeal for information. 'Ex-client,' Jenessa said, trying hard to sound as though it didn't matter in the least that she had been unceremoniously fired in full view of several friends and acquaintances. 'He's done me a favor, actually—I could do with a few days off.' She smiled at Ruth's brother. 'How are you, Dougie? Job going well?'

Ten minutes later she stalked into Ryan's kitchen. Her temper, far from subsiding on the drive home, seemed to have gathered momentum. Handsome, she fumed inwardly, throwing the keys to her van on the table. Rough-hewn. Huh! Rude, chauvinistic and ignorant would be a more accurate description of Mr Finn Marston.

Ryan was sitting at the table painting a duck decoy. Matters weren't improved when he said, after scanning her features, 'Well, well... looks like this Marston fella woke you up a bit—haven't seen so much colour in your cheeks since you were a kid with sunburn. What's up, Jenny?'

'Ryan,' she said, 'don't you ever again neglect to warn a client that he's getting a female guide. A woman. One of the so-called weaker sex. Do you hear me?'

As she yanked a chair back and sat down, kicking off her loafers, Ryan daubed jade-green on the teal's wing feathers. 'Wanted a man, did he?'

'However did you guess? Did he wait to see my references? Was he interested enough to ask if I knew the area he wants to go? Can a caribou outrun a black bear?'

'Never knew one that could,' Ryan said, his mouth twitching. 'It don't sound like the two of you hit it off.'

'I hope he ends up with the worst guide in the entire province. Someone like Larry, who'll drop him off in the woods and then go and get drunk. I hope the mosquitoes carry him away. I hope he gets treed by a moose. I hope he falls in a bog in his nice leather hiking boots.'

'So what did he look like?'

She mimicked Ruth's mother, batting her lashes and simpering, 'Tall, dark and handsome. Rough-hewn. That duck decoy's handsomer than he was.'

Ryan gave the decoy a complacent appraisal. 'He sure got under your skin.'

Ryan, she realized belatedly, was thoroughly enjoying her show of temper; she was normally a very tolerant woman, a trait that stood her in good stead in the woods. The last thing she needed was Ryan speculating why one man had disrupted her composure, especially in view of yesterday's conversation. 'I needed a few days off anyway,' she said, trying to modulate her voice. 'We could finish papering the kitchen.'

One wall had been papered in the spring, before fishing season started. 'Good idea... in the meantime, seein' as how you're unemployed, you could make me a coffee. And don't skimp on the sugar.'

'No coffee unless you promise you'll tell everyone who phones for a guide that my name is Jenessa and that I'm not a man!'

'Guess I'll git my own coffee,' Ryan drawled.

Raising her brows—for when had she ever been able to make Ryan do something he didn't want to do?—Jenessa got up and reached for the coffee in the cupboard.

CHAPTER TWO

AT NINE-THIRTY the next morning Jenessa was standing on the second from the top rung of a step-ladder in the kitchen. The radio was blaring a lachrymose ballad about a cowpoke who had lost his one true love. It was a warm day; her brief blue shorts and ribbed vest top in an eye-catching shade of yellow had been chosen with coolness in mind rather than modesty. Draped in wet folds of wallpaper, she was seriously questioning her sanity. She hated wallpapering. Always had. She might be exceedingly neat-fingered when it came to starting a fire from birchbark and shreds of wood in the middle of a downpour in the forest, but when it came to straight edges, plumb lines and recurring patterns she was a dud.

Ryan had ordered the wallpaper from a nature company; it was replete with partridge, loons and owls on a gloomy green and blue background. She had to match the loon chick under her left palm with the one in the preceding row—which meant she was going to have to decapitate the topmost row of partridge.

As the old pine floorboards creaked behind her, she said irritably, 'Turn the radio down, would you, Ryan, and pass me the knife? If I hadn't been in such a foul mood last night, I would never have suggested doing this—and don't say it serves me right for losing my temper.'

A hand reached up with a yellow-handled knife. It was a tanned, smoothly muscled hand with long, lean fingers; it was definitely not Ryan's hand. With a shriek of alarm Jenessa twisted on the step-ladder, which gave an unsettling lurch. '*You*! What are you doing here?'

Finn Marston grabbed the ladder with his free hand, holding it firm, and said, 'From all reports I gather you're more to be depended on in the wilderness than you'd appear to be at the top of this ladder. Where's your father?'

'Father?' she repeated idiotically. 'My father's been dead since I was thirteen.'

'Ryan's not your father, then? But you live with him?' he rapped.

In the morning light, shaven, his hair shining with cleanliness, Finn Marston did indeed qualify as handsome, Jenessa thought grudgingly. More than handsome. There was something quintessentially male about him: he made her think of the proud stance of a caribou stag out on the barrens.

Although he still looked tired out. The kind of tiredness that one night's sleep did nothing to allay.

She said flatly, 'My living arrangements are none of your business. Now if you'll excuse me, I've got to get this piece in place before it dries.'

She took the knife from him with the very tips of her fingers, adjusted the strip of wallpaper so that the loon chicks matched up and sliced the top of the paper level with the edge of the ceiling. The row of partridge heads slithered to the floor. Bending, Jenessa picked up the sponge from the top step of the ladder and started smoothing the wallpaper flat. Finn Marston was still holding the ladder, so close behind her that as the ballad ended, predictably, at the graveside, she could hear his breathing.

She tried to ignore him; when that didn't work, she waited for him to say something, anything, the silence scraping on her nerves as she bit back any number of questions of her own, none of them polite. When there was not a single air bubble left under the damp paper and she knew she could delay facing him no longer, she turned awkwardly on the ladder and sat down on the top step, her bare feet curving round a lower rung. This put her several inches above him, a position she liked. She hadn't known Finn Marston long but she already knew she needed every advantage she could get.

She might be aware of her advantage; it hadn't occurred to her that the smooth curves of her legs and the shadowed hollow between her breasts were now practically under his nose.

His face changed, marred by a cynicism so intense that Jenessa was bewildered. Then, with a jolt, she realized what he was thinking. He thought she was posing for him deliberately. What was the phrase she had used at Ruth's? Flaunting her sexuality.

Laughter bubbled in her chest, so far from the truth was he, nor did she bother hiding it. Not moving an inch, she watched as his cynicism was gradually replaced by a puzzlement too obvious to be anything but genuine. She had knocked him off balance, she thought, and wondered with a cynicism all her own how many women were able to do that. Not many, she'd be willing to bet.

From her vantage point she was only a couple of feet away from him. His face, close up, interested her in spite of herself. Over the last few years she had become fairly adept at reading character, actively trying to develop this talent as one of her survival mechanisms in the male-dominated environment in which she worked. If she applied her talents to Finn Marston's face, what did she see?

Overwhelming exhaustion first, an exhaustion ground into the tightly held jaw and dark-shadowed eyes. He had been driven unmercifully for far too long; and she suspected that he himself was the one to have plied the whip, for he would do to himself what he would not allow others to do. Yet there was a formidable intelligence informing his features, as well as the will-power she had had a taste of last night. His eyes, deep-set, were indeed the same navy blue as Stephen's; however, while Stephen's were lustrous with the innocence of the very young, Finn Marston's were guarded and wary. His mouth was a firm, ungiving line. She was suddenly visited with the urge to see it smile.

Her survey had taken her only a few seconds. 'Now,' Jenessa said coldly, 'perhaps you wouldn't mind explaining why you walked in this house without knocking and without an invitation?'

'The door was wide open and the radio was making so much noise you didn't hear me knock,' he said. 'Where's Ryan?'

'He went out to the shed to get a hammer and nails. Ryan frequently gets waylaid, but I've no doubt he'll return sooner or later. Why are you here?'

'What's his relationship to you?'

'Of the two questions, I'd say mine was the more relevant.'

'Would you, now?'

'Yes,' she said sharply, 'I would. Quite frankly, Mr Marston, after last night I don't care if I ever set eyes on you again.'

He said evenly, not a trace of apology in his tone, 'You were right—there aren't any other guides available. Or, to be accurate, there were two, both of whom I figured were capable of guiding me from the motel to the nearest bar and no further. You'll also be glad to know that everyone I spoke to sang your praises. Short of Ryan, I gather you're the best guide in the area. So I came here to see if I could rehire you. You or Ryan.'

'You'll have to ask Ryan yourself. I, as you can see, am otherwise engaged.'

'A thousand a week, all expenses paid.'

Jenessa blinked; she had never been paid that much in her life. 'And how much would you pay a man? Two thousand?'

'I'd pay him what I'd pay you.' He paused and added tersely, 'I'm sorry I went off the deep end last night. My only excuse is that I was jet-lagged and just about asleep on my feet.'

'Which is exactly when our true selves emerge,' she said promptly.

His fingers tightened around the ladder. 'I'm not going to grovel. You heard my offer. Take it or leave it.'

'Oh, I'll——'

The porch door slammed shut and Ryan bellowed, 'Jenny, we got a visitor; there was a cab sittin' out in the yard. Who do you suppose came to see us in a——? Well, who've we got here?'

Ryan, thought Jenessa wryly, did not look his best. He had a baseball cap jammed backward on his head, his shirt was paint-spattered and one knee was out of his jeans. He was carrying an unpainted decoy instead of the hammer and nails. She said sweetly, 'Someone who wants to hire you as a guide, Ryan. Allow me to introduce Mr Finn Marston . . . Thaddeus Ryan.'

She sat back on the ladder, her face lit with an amusement that Finn Marston could not have missed. Ryan grinned at the other man. 'Couldn't get anyone else, eh? Figured that's what would happen.'

'The joke's on me,' Finn Marston said tightly. 'Maybe we could all have a good laugh and then get down to business.'

'Oh, Jenessa'll go. She hates wallpaperin',' Ryan said, plunking the decoy down on the table.

'I will not!'

'Fifteen hundred,' Finn Marston said. 'And that's my last offer.'

Angrier than she could ever remember being in her life, Jenessa choked, 'You seem to think that this is about money, Mr Marston—that you can buy me. Well, you can't! You embarrassed and insulted me in front of a group of my friends last night, and nothing you've said or done today has caused me to forgive you. Now, if you'll kindly let go of this ladder, I'll put up the next piece of wallpaper. Ask Ryan to guide you—his hide's tougher than mine.'

'Can't,' said Ryan. 'Takin' Grace to the bingo social on the weekend.'

There was a small silence, during which Finn Marston's gaze locked with Jenessa's and Ryan filled the kettle. Hugging her bare knees, Jenessa refused to let her eyes drop. Consequently she was the first to see in her adversary's face something that could have been the beginnings of respect. He let go of the ladder and ran his fingers through his hair. 'How about if I take back everything I've said so far and start over? Will you listen? At least give me a fair hearing?'

'I might,' she said, raising her chin.

It was not an overwhelming endorsement; but plainly he realized it was all he was going to get. He paused, searching for words. 'I live in a man's world, Jenessa Reed. It's a tough and dangerous world, and I'm at the top of the heap—I'm the one who gives the orders and

I expect instant obedience. Because if you don't obey you can end up dead. I've had very little to do with women the last few years, and I've never had a whole lot of respect for them. So the thought of being guided through the wilderness by a woman didn't—and still doesn't—fill me with joy. Although I was tired last night and less than diplomatic, my feelings are the same today. I'd much prefer you to be a man.'

He gave her a smile that was a mere movement of his lips. 'It would also seem that I have no choice—you're the only guide available. So I'm asking you to reconsider.'

'You're honest,' she said slowly, 'I'll give you that.'

'I've never had much use for lying. Honesty saves trouble in the long run.'

A pragmatist rather than a moralist, Jenessa thought. The workings of Finn Marston's mind were beginning to interest her rather more than she liked; simultaneously her intuition was warning her to run a mile. She said, 'I'll be equally honest, then. I'm not really in a position where I can afford to turn down a week's work; the winters are long around here. But I won't take a penny more than seven hundred a week, and if we're in a tight spot out in the woods and I tell you to do something I'll expect *you* to obey *me*. No questions asked. We can have a lovely argument afterwards about male dominance—but at the time you'll do what I say.'

'Because it's your territory.'

'That's right.' She smiled suddenly, a smile that lit up her face. 'I've never lost a client yet, and I don't plan to start with you.'

While he didn't smile back, his face did relax slightly. 'Eight hundred a week.'

'Seven.'

The kettle screamed on the stove and Ryan banged three pottery mugs on the table. Spooning instant coffee into them, he said, 'Quit fightin', you two. If you're hell-bent on overpayin' her, Marston, tip her at the end of the trip.' His grin was frankly malicious. 'Let's drink to the partnership, eh? One thing's for sure—I doubt it'll be dull.'

Finn Marston turned away from her and Jenessa scrambled down the ladder. Somehow, in the last ten minutes, she had agreed to go to an undisclosed destination for an unknown length of time with a man who set off all her alarm bells. She put a healthy dollop of honey in her mug and watched as Ryan sloshed in the boiling water. 'You haven't told me yet where we're going or for how long you've hired me, Mr Marston,' she said.

'I've got all the maps back at the motel. Maybe we could go there next and I can show you; it'd be simpler than trying to explain it here. I don't have any idea how long it'll take. I do know I don't have any time to waste—I probably shouldn't be here at all. So we'll be moving as fast as we can.'

'At least tell me if we're going into the interior.'

'That's the understatement of the year,' he said, his voice holding an edge of bitterness.

'Do you have knee-high rubber boots?'

'Not with me.'

'We'll go to a supplier in town and get you a pair,' she said. 'Leather hiking boots are useless in a bog.'

'All right,' he said.

For the first time she saw a flash of humor glint in his eyes. She chuckled, beguiled by the way it had lightened his features. 'Instant obedience,' she remarked. 'You learn fast.'

'You're the only guide available—right?' he said drily. Turning to Ryan, he asked, 'What kind of duck is that?'

Ryan loved to talk about his decoys and was soon launched on one of his many hunting stories. Jenessa drank her coffee then pushed back from the table. 'I'm going to change; I'll be back in a few minutes,' she said.

Ten minutes later, showered and dressed in jeans, a plain short-sleeved safari shirt and sandals, she was back in the kitchen, her over-long hair clinging damply to her neck. Finn Marston stood up as soon as she entered. 'Thanks for the coffee, Ryan,' he said.

'Any time.' Ryan gave an uncouth cackle. 'Don't run from a black bear and don't let the stouts bite ya.'

Jenessa raised her brows and led the way out of the kitchen. 'A black bear can run forty-five miles an hour out on the barrens,' she explained, leading the way to her red van. 'So there's not much point in trying to run away from one. And a stout's the Newfoundland version of a deer fly—unceasingly hungry and oblivious to any brand of fly dope that I've ever tried. They've been known to drive caribou crazy in the early summer.'

'Are you trying to discourage me?'

'And talk myself out of seven hundred a week?' she said limpidly, starting the motor and steering the van between the potholes in Ryan's driveway.

'You don't work just for money.'

'I work because I love being outdoors,' Jenessa said with sudden intensity. 'I couldn't bear to be cooped up in an office all day.'

'I suffer from the same problem,' he said. 'What's your relationship to Ryan?'

His change of subject made her edgy. 'He was my father's best friend, and he taught me just about everything I know about the woods. I've lived with him since I was sixteen.'

'But your father died when you were thirteen. Did you live with your mother for the next three years?'

That three years had been the worst time of Jenessa's life. Braking at a stop sign, she said carefully, 'Would you be asking me these kinds of questions—personal ones, I mean—if I were a man?'

'You're not.'

She crossed the street, driving past a row of small bungalows and deciding that two could play that game. 'Why don't you have much respect for women?' she asked.

He gave a short laugh. 'There are no flies on you, stout or otherwise. By the way, I didn't bring any fly dope—maybe we could buy some.'

'I've got lots. The flies aren't that bad now; we've had a few cold nights.' She swung round a corner, aware that he hadn't answered her question any more than she had answered his. 'We'll get the boots from my friend Stevie; he's the only one in town who carries them. Have you got rain gear, Mr Marston?'

'As we're going to be spending the next few days together, why don't we go with Finn and Jenessa?' he said impatiently.

Normally Jenessa preferred being on a first-name basis. But for a reason she couldn't fathom, hearing her name on Finn's lips made her feel as though he was laying claim to some part of her, a part that was strictly her own. Chiding herself for being overly imaginative, she said coolly, 'Fine. Rain gear?'

He nodded. Efficiently she ran through a list of personal gear he'd need, finishing, 'We supply tents and sleeping-bags and all the food. Here we are...Ruth's home, by the look of it, but not Stevie.'

Ruth greeted them cheerfully, clearly impressed by Jenessa's latest client. She led them to the room in the basement where she and Stevie sold a wide array of hunting and fishing equipment, and pulled out a stack of boxes. 'Your size should be here,' she said to Finn. 'Try them on and feel free to walk around outdoors in them.'

As he slipped his feet into the first pair of rubber boots, Ruth remarked with rather overdone casualness, 'Jenessa, I was just talking to Marylou—her ten-thirty appointment was cancelled; you should take a run over.'

'I don't have the time,' Jenessa said shortly. As Finn stood up, she knelt at his feet, pressing on the toes of the boots to see how they fit, her shirt pulled tight over the slim line of her back. 'They seem a little small,' she said dubiously, glancing up at him. 'If we do any amount of walking, it's really important to get a good fit.'

With a directness that no longer surprised her, he said, 'Who's Marylou?'

'The hairdresser next door,' she answered repressively. 'I think you should try a half-size larger.'

He did so, and said with a satisfied grunt, 'They feel better—maybe I will walk outside in them, if that's okay.' The smile he gave Ruth would have charmed the birds from the trees, Jenessa thought sourly; she got the tail end of it as he added, 'Come with me, Jenessa; you can probably tell if I've got the right ones better than I can.'

She trailed up the steps behind him. He walked across the front lawn, glanced at Marylou's sign and wrapped his fingers around Jenessa's elbow. 'If I've got to take to the woods with a woman, I'd at least prefer her to look like one,' he said, and steered her unceremoniously toward Marylou's side-door.

Jenessa's jaw had dropped. She snapped it shut, dug her heels into the grass and sputtered, '*What* do you think you're doing?'

'Getting you a haircut. Maybe she'll do mine at the same time.'

'You can shave your head for all I care,' Jenessa stormed, tugging fruitlessly at his fingers. 'My hair's fine as it is and Ruth's mother, who lives right across the street, is undoubtedly glued to the window watching us. This'll be all over town by evening.'

'Then you'd better stop struggling, hadn't you?' he said.

He was a good five inches taller than she and stronger by far. Disconcertingly strong, she thought with a quiver of unease. 'What do you do for your living?' she asked.

'If I'm not allowed to ask personal questions, neither are you. Come along.'

One thing Jenessa had learned in her life was when to give up fighting the odds. Vowing to herself that no matter where she and Finn Marston went she'd walk him through every bog she could find until he begged for mercy, she stalked into Marylou's beauty parlor.

Marylou favored frilly curtains, crocheted mats and artificial flowers; Finn's big body looked totally out of place. Marylou herself was plump and pretty, her forget-me-not-blue eyes concealing a shrewd grasp of business. With frigid politeness Jenessa said, 'Marylou, this is Finn Marston—I'm guiding for him. He wants a haircut.'

Finn had been looking around with interest. He pointed to a photo of a woman's head that had been mounted on the wall and said, 'Could you give Jenessa that cut, Marylou?'

'Sure I could—it'd look real nice on her.'

Jenessa glared at him. 'He's the one who needs the haircut. Not me.'

Marylou said amiably, 'I'm free until lunchtime, so I can do both of you. You first, Jenessa; you just sit down right over here.'

Finn said equally amiably, 'I think she cut it with a hacksaw last time.'

Torn between fury and a crazy urge to laugh, Jenessa said, 'What's the matter, Finn—having problems with your masculinity? Got to assert yourself now because I'm the one who'll be giving the orders once we leave town?'

Marylou was swathing her in a plastic cape at the sink. He said succinctly, 'You've got it wrong—*you* have problems with your femininity. I'll be back in a few minutes.'

Ryan, Ruth and now Finn—it was too much. But Marylou had turned on the tap full force and Finn was striding out of the door in his new rubber boots. Jenessa leaned back and closed her eyes, any number of clever rebuttals seething in her brain. She paid scant attention as Marylou shampooed and rinsed her hair, then combed it out and started to cut. Finn Marston had better not push her too far, she thought darkly; she hadn't signed any contracts, so she could resign any time she liked and leave him in the lurch.

He didn't think she looked like a woman. Whatever that meant.

One thing was sure: he hadn't intended it as a compliment.

CHAPTER THREE

MARYLOU chattered on about the plot twists in the daily soap operas, keeping herself between Jenessa and the mirror. The blow-drier wafted warm air around Jenessa's ears. Then Marylou brushed her hair in place, snipping a few loose ends with her scissors. She swivelled Jenessa round to face the mirror, saying with immense satisfaction, 'Ever since I took that last seminar I've been wanting to get my hands on your hair, love—not bad, eh?'

Stunned, Jenessa looked at the stranger in the glass. Her hair was now tapered over her ears, emphasizing the slender length of her neck and the shape of her eyes with their brilliant green irises, and bringing her cheekbones into new prominence; wisps of hair, polished like the cherrywood to which Ruth had compared it, softened her forehead and clung to her nape. 'It doesn't even look like me,' she said stupidly.

The door creaked open. Then another reflection joined hers in the mirror: the man who was the cause of this. He was staring straight at her, dark blue eyes meeting green. He looked, she thought in utter panic, like a hunter who had caught sight of his prey.

'Looks nice, doesn't it?' Marylou said complacently. 'I won't charge you full price, dear, because it gave me the chance to try something new. Did you say you wanted a cut, Mr Marston?'

With a palpable effort Finn dragged his gaze from Jenessa's. 'Just a trim,' he said.

Jenessa got up, threw a couple of bills on the counter and croaked, 'I'll be at Ruth's.' She ran outside and across the lawn, feeling the breeze on her bare neck, and had she been asked she couldn't have said what—or whom—she was fleeing.

In Ruth's kitchen she skidded to a halt. Ruth, Stephen and Ruth's mother Alice were all in the kitchen; Alice was the last person Jenessa wanted to see. If her brain had been working, she thought frantically, she would have realized Alice would have rushed straight over to Ruth's on a fact-finding mission. Ruth said, 'Jenessa—your hair is *gorgeous*!'

'My, my,' Alice said coyly, 'never knew you to change your looks for a man, Jenessa. He must be someone pretty special.'

Jenessa could not begin to answer this. She reached out for Stephen, cuddling him and playing with his pudgy little fingers. 'How's the new tooth, sweetie?' she babbled. 'I'd love a cup of tea, Ruth. Stevie's getting home tonight, isn't that what you told me?'

'No,' said Ruth, 'I never told you that. He's not back until next week.' Taking pity on her friend, she said firmly, 'Mum, why don't you run home and fetch us a few doughnuts to go with our tea? You make the best doughnuts in town.'

When Alice came back a few minutes later, Jenessa was ladling cereal into Stephen's mouth and Ruth was determinedly discussing the local by-election. But Alice was not so easily discouraged. Into the first pause in the conversation she said, 'Looked to me like you and that handsome Finn Marston were having a tiff on the front lawn, Jenessa—I hear you're going into the woods with him, though.'

She managed to make this latter phrase sound thoroughly clandestine. 'I'm guiding him, yes,' Jenessa replied. 'Oops, Stephen, we missed that one.'

'After all this time—when I'd just about given up on you, dearie, I might as well tell you the truth—I do believe you're finally falling in love,' Alice crowed.

The spoon dropped with a clatter on to the high tray, cereal spattered Jenessa's shirt and she said with more force than wisdom, 'I'm *not* in love with him; don't be silly, Alice! He's a rude, chauvinistic, controlling——'

She broke off, for Finn Marston had just opened the screen door and must have heard every word she'd said. Feeling a strong urge to burst into tears, she wailed, 'I don't know what's the matter with me—I'm never rude to my clients—it's one of my unbreakable rules... and I've got cereal all down my clean shirt! Wallpapering would be better than this.'

Finn beat Ruth to the sink, took the cloth from the dishrack and wet it under the tap. Then he advanced on Jenessa. 'Hold still,' he said.

'Oh, no,' she said warmly, 'I'm quite capable of wiping my own shirt, thank you.'

'You're like a hedgehog,' he said. 'All prickles.'

'There aren't any hedgehogs in Newfoundland.'

'There's one right here in the kitchen.'

She yanked the cloth from his hand and scrubbed at her shirt. 'I'm never rude to clients and I never go to beauty parlors,' she muttered. 'I wish I knew what was going on here.'

'Do you really not know?' Finn said with sudden intentness.

She glanced up. His hair, newly trimmed and entirely civilized, made his features look all the more rough-hewn; she had no idea what he was thinking. 'No,' she said.

He said quietly, speaking to her alone, 'Then I'll tell you . . . I was in Tunisia once and I found an old ceramic pot buried by a dried-up pond. The pot was stained and dirty and filled with mud. So I took it back to the camp and washed it very carefully and polished it with a soft cloth—and then I saw that it had an exquisite design of tiny green birds and marsh reeds etched all around the lip. It was very beautiful.' He looked at her, his dark blue eyes fathomless. 'That was why I wanted your hair cut.'

A tide of hot color swept across Jenessa's cheeks. For several seconds she was literally speechless. Then she whispered, 'Beautiful? *Me*?'

'Jenessa, where have you been all your life? Yes, beautiful.'

Alice gave a sigh of repletion. 'My, oh, my, I wish I'd had my video camera for that,' she said soulfully. 'Better than *Another World*.'

Jenessa scarcely heard her. Like a woman in a dream she walked over to the little mirror that hung over the sink and stared at herself. She had no need of make-up, she thought. Her cheeks were flushed, her eyes shining; she looked as fully alive as a brightly colored butterfly dancing from flower to flower in the sunlight.

Behind her Finn said abruptly, 'We'd better go. We've got to figure out our route, and I need some kind of time frame so I can phone my company. Thanks for the boots, Ruth—coming, Jenessa?'

Trying to gather her wits, Jenessa dropped a kiss on Stephen's fluffy hair, hugged Ruth and Alice, whose eyes were almost popping out of her head, and walked outside to the van. Driving gave her something to focus on, and

Finn said not a word as they crossed town to the motel. She parked in front of his unit and followed him into the room. The door clicked shut behind them.

His luggage was neatly stashed against the wall, the blue shirt he had been wearing last night was hanging over the back of one of the chairs and a bundle of papers and maps had been thrown on the bed. The maps seemed to steady her; she knew about maps, knew how to read them and transpose the thin lines on the paper to the actual contours of the land. She took a deep breath and said with commendable matter-of-factness, 'Show me where you want to go.'

He sat down on the edge of the bed, unfolding a map of the whole province as well as two detailed topographical maps. 'We'll fly by helicopter into this lodge,' he said, 'I have connections with the oil companies, and I can get a 'copter any time I want one.'

Casually Jenessa sat down beside him, one leg tucked under her, following the line of his finger to a lake well south of the highway. Her eyes widened in dismay. Caribou Lake. Of all the thousands of lakes in Newfoundland, Finn Marston wanted to go to Caribou Lake.

'The lodge is called Caribou Outfitters. Run by a guy called Lloyd MacDonald—calls himself Mac; I've already talked to him. Do you know the area at all?'

'I know it very well,' she said raggedly.

He shot a quick look at her. 'You've been there before?'

'Many times.' With at least partial truth she said, 'I used to work for Mac. A couple of years ago. I don't see why you need me if you're going to his lodge; he has his own guides.'

'I'm only using the lodge as a base. This is where I really want to go.'

With true incredulity Jenessa watched his finger move still further south into a network of lakes and still waters that she could have traced on the map with her eyes shut. In a cracked voice she said, 'That's Hilchey land—what do you want to go there for?'

'You're familiar with it?'

'He's dead—old Mr Hilchey. He died six months ago. Why do you want to see his property?'

'I asked you a question, Jenessa—are you familiar with that land?'

She gave a short, unamused laugh. 'I've walked every ridge and barren, and canoed every waterway from Caribou River to Indian Brook.' And if she had ever hated anyone in her life, it had been George Hilchey.

Finn spread out one of the topographical maps. 'It's a huge area; how could you know it so well?'

The names on the map jumped out at her. Osprey Falls, Beothuck Pond, Juniper Lake. Names and places that she had discovered as a child and loved with all the passionate intensity of a child. To the east lay Spruce Pond, where she had lived with her father for thirteen years on a tiny cove in sight of two tree-clad islands; her eyes shied away from it, for she had never once gone back there and now doubted that she ever would. She said, hard-voiced, 'Why do you want to go there, Finn?'

His mouth tightened. 'Curiosity,' he said.

'That's no kind of an answer!'

'It's all the answer you're going to get. George Hilchey used to have a summer place here on this lake—I want to visit it, and check out the area while I'm there.'

'I wish you'd told me this last night,' she said tautly. 'It would have saved both of us a lot of trouble. For reasons that are nothing to do with you, I can't possibly go there.'

His eyes narrowed, the force of his will-power like a blast of cold wind. 'You'll go,' he said.

'One of Mac's guides will take you in—you'd have to go by canoe.'

'*Canoe*?'

'It's the only way to get there.'

'I've never been in a canoe in my life!'

'A new experience for you,' she said ironically.

'Jenessa, in case you haven't heard of them, there's a marvellous twentieth-century invention called a float plane. It lands on lakes. This place is riddled with lakes.'

'You see these crosses on the lake? Those are rocks. Big rocks. They don't bother marking all the little ones. Plus there are deadheads in those waters—submerged logs—from the days of the log jams on the rivers. No pilot in his right mind is going to risk a float plane on those waters.'

'We'll take the helicopter in.'

'No clearings. Hilchey's summer place hasn't been used in twenty years—the alders will have taken over.'

'For God's sake!' Finn exploded. 'It'll take days to get in there by canoe.'

'A week, I'd say.'

'Then another week to get out—I haven't got that kind of time to waste.'

She shrugged, tamping down a mixture of emotions too complicated to analyze. 'Have the helicopter fly low over the land; that should satisfy your curiosity. It'll cost you a small fortune, mind you. Although,' she added with a touch of malice, 'you'll be saving seven hundred a week.'

'But you're saying the 'copter can't land at the summer house.' He got up from the bed, prowling round the room like a caged bear. 'Couldn't you get there in less than a week?'

She shook her head. 'That's back country...a strong wind can easily hold you up for a couple of days. Besides, if your guide has any sense, he'll keep you two or three days at the lodge learning the essentials of canoeing before you set out. There's whitewater on some of those rivers, and you're miles from anywhere.'

He glared at her. 'So now it's three weeks!'

'Finn,' she said curiously, 'how long is it since you've taken a holiday?'

'I forget.'

'The wilderness has its own time scheme. Dawn and dusk, winds and rain...you can't force it or control it.'

'I don't think you understand—I run a multi-million-dollar business,' he snapped. 'Big-league stuff.'

'Then go back to it and forget about George Hilchey's summer house,' she said indifferently.

He thrust his hands in the pockets of his jeans. 'It's a wonder to me that none of your clients has ever shot *you* rather than the moose.'

Jenessa laughed, abandoning their argument, because after all it was nothing to do with her how Finn got to the old summer house. 'One or two of them have contemplated it, I'm sure.'

Her eyes were dancing, her pose on the big bed unselfconsciously graceful. Finn took a step toward her, halted and said levelly, 'Excuse me a minute.'

He went to the phone, punched a great many numbers, eventually said a few phrases in a language unknown to

Jenessa, and finally rapped, 'Jonah? Finn here. What's up?'

Jenessa smoothed the map flat, fighting back a wave of nostalgia for the woods and waters of her childhood, and heard Finn say, 'You did? On the second attempt? It fit the flange? Then it was worthwhile doing the trial run... When do you think you'll pull out? You'll join them in Venezuela by Thursday? Yeah...I'm thinking of taking two or three weeks, Jonah. By the sound of it you're coping just fine without me. If you need anything while I'm away you'll have to go via Moswell's helicopter and a place called Caribou Lodge; the 'copter pilot will know where that is. You did a fine job. Get Brian to keep on top of all the finances, won't you? Okay, all the best.'

He put down the receiver and turned back to Jenessa. 'What time can we be ready to leave?'

'I'm not going!'

'You agreed to guide for me. You can't go back on that.'

'You mean you can fire me but I can't quit?'

Without emphasis Finn said, 'You wouldn't want me putting the word round that you broke a contract, would you? Even if it was only a verbal one.'

Jenessa got a lot of her work by word of mouth. In a surge of pure rage she said, 'Is this the way you act in the business world? No wonder you made it to the top.'

'I do what it takes. You're going to guide me to the Hilchey place, Jenessa—I won't take no for an answer.' He gave her the faintest of smiles. 'Anyway, I've just agreed to take my first vacation in over five years—you can't let me down now.'

With utter clarity Jenessa thought, I have a choice here. I can stay home and wallpaper the kitchen. Safe and ordinary and boring, and if Finn blackens my name I'll survive. Or I can risk going back to the place where I grew up. Seeing it from the perspective of an adult. I'm twice as old as I was when I left . . . I'm not thirteen any more, raw with pain and filled with fear. Maybe the old magic will have gone. Maybe it'll be just another place, nothing special.

Maybe it's time I laid that particular ghost to rest.

'Why are you so interested in the Hilchey land?' she demanded. 'Are you some kind of high-powered lawyer settling the estate? Although you don't act like any lawyer I ever knew.'

'Not once in my life have I ever contemplated joining the legal profession,' Finn said pithily. 'I only wish I understood why that land's so important to you—why you won't tell me what your connection is with it.'

She couldn't possibly explain it to him. As she shook her head, her green eyes wary, he said, 'I'll ask Ryan.'

'Not if you value living, you won't.'

'I've stepped into something, haven't I?' he said slowly. 'Something pretty major as far as you're concerned. Maybe Mac will tell me when we get to the lodge.'

'Mac will tell you exactly what he thinks you want to hear—he's a master at that.'

'And to think,' Finn remarked, 'that I almost didn't come here because I figured I'd be bored.' In one of the swift shifts of topic that she had almost come to expect of him, he added, 'Are you afraid to spend two or three weeks alone with me?'

She raised her chin. 'I've never been afraid of a man in my life.'

'There are some you should be frightened of.'

'You're not one of them,' Jenessa said, and wondered if she was speaking the truth. If her behaviour of the last eighteen hours was anything to go by, perhaps she should be afraid.

'So what time are we leaving?' Finn repeated softly.

One last chance to see the land she had roamed as a girl. To choose risk over safety. Biting her lip, she muttered, 'Ryan will organize the gear but I'll have to look after the food... I'd say by four. I'll talk to Mac and tell him we'll be there in time for supper.'

She was staring down at the map and missed the triumph that raced across Finn's face. He made another phone call, arranging for the helicopter to take them to the lodge. Then he sat down on the bed again. 'So, Jenessa Reed,' he said, 'we're on. We're spending the next two weeks together.'

The choice, she had known all along, hadn't only been a matter of the land. Her mouth dry, she said, 'As employer and employee.'

'We're already more than that, and you know it.'

Certainly she had never been so outspoken to any of her other clients. 'That's all we are,' she said stubbornly.

With unexpected violence Finn said, 'I don't have a clue what's going on here! But I'll tell you one thing—you're totally unlike any other woman I've ever been with. Nor, for some reason, can I believe that I only met you last night.'

Inwardly terrified, outwardly composed, Jenessa quipped, 'You feel as if we've been arguing forever?'

Some of the tension eased in his face. 'You're certainly the most contentious woman I've ever met.'

'But you said yourself the sample was small,' she answered gently, and stood up. 'I'd better go; I've got a lot to do. I'll be back here at quarter to four.'

Finn stood up too, his body moving with a lazy grace. Very deliberately he held out his hand. 'I'm glad we're going to be together,' he said.

She could not, without adding bad manners to contentiousness, refuse to shake hands with him. Reluctantly she stretched out her own. His grip was firm, his palm warm against hers. She looked down, in one glance seeing the lean length of his fingers with their well-kept nails and the dusting of dark hair on the back of his hand, where the bones and sinews moved under the tanned skin. His wristwatch with its new leather strap looked expensive. His forearm was tanned as well, corded with muscle. Then the faint tang of his aftershave drifted to her nostrils, and underlying it she caught something far more elemental and more powerful: the scent of the man himself.

She glanced up, her nerves as alert as if she had just sighted a fresh bear track on the trail, her senses acutely aware of the sound of his breathing and the warmth of his body across the space that separated them. She had touched a man before, of course she had. But never had she felt such an instinctive vigilance, so total and instant an involvement; with a lurch of her heart she found herself comparing it with the strange bond that united the hunter and the hunted. Pulling her hand free, her green eyes bewildered, she muttered, 'Two weeks could be a very long time.'

'It'll be as long as we need,' Finn said cryptically. 'I'll see you later.'

She hurried outdoors into the sunshine, wondering what she had gotten herself into. She had told the truth when she'd said she'd never been afraid of a man; even Mac had never really frightened her.

But Finn Marston was different. Dauntingly different.

He wouldn't take no for an answer. And he thought she was beautiful.

CHAPTER FOUR

THE next few hours were hectically busy for Jenessa. She drove straight home and told Ryan about the proposed trip to the property that George Hilchey had owned. As Ryan raised bushy white brows, she warned, 'I don't want to talk about it and I swear if you so much as breathe a word to Finn about my connection with that land I'll move out and I'll never come back.'

This was indeed a dire threat. Ryan solemnly ran a dirty finger across his throat and said, 'You want me to load up the two backpacks?'

'That'd be a great help. Water tablets, flashlights, tents, tarp... you know what we need, Ryan. The food's going to take a bit of organizing; I'll head out to the grocery store after I call Mac.'

She got through on the radio-phone to Caribou Lodge on the first try. 'Mac? Jenessa Reed here. I'll be arriving at the lodge around five-thirty today with a man called Finn Marston; can you put him up for a couple of nights?'

There was a fractional pause. 'So he hired you, did he? I didn't have a guide free.'

She knew Mac well; beneath the innocuous words he was angry. 'As you've already spoken to him, then you know what he wants,' she said calmly. 'We'll be canoeing to the old Hilchey place, but I'll want to be around the lodge for two or three days first; he's never been in a canoe before. Any problem with that?'

'He can have a room in the lodge. You can go in the guides' cabin.'

'We can rent a canoe?'

'A seventeen-foot wood and canvas.'

'Great. We'll bring our own food and gear. Thanks, Mac.'

'See you,' he grunted.

Mac didn't want them there. She'd bet her bottom dollar on it. More undercurrents, Jenessa thought, and for the life of her couldn't understand what they might be. Yes, she'd turned Mac down two years ago. But they'd met since then and he'd been at his most charming, as though to show her that he couldn't care less. Frowning, she started on the grocery list.

At quarter to four she stuffed the last pair of clean socks into one of the side-pockets of her backpack. Ryan had already loaded Finn's into the van; although she hadn't had the time to check its contents, Ryan had been packing for long trips most of his life and wouldn't be likely to have forgotten anything. Paddles, life-vests, the Duluth packs with the food... they were all in the van, too.

'Move it, Jenny,' Ryan hollered.

She swung the pack on her back and hurried outside, and they arrived at the motel at five to four. Finn was standing outside, his duffel bag and haversack at his feet. He put his gear in the back where Ryan was sitting and sat in the front beside Jenessa. 'We're late,' he said.

'The helicopter won't go without us,' she responded evenly, and swung out into the traffic.

When they got to the hangar, the oil-company helicopter was parked on the tarmac. Jenessa had met the pilot before, a man in his forties by the name of Wally. She introduced Finn and they started loading gear in the helicopter. Crouched in the rear, she said, 'Could you pass up those two canvas bags, Finn? Careful, they're heavy; they've got all our food.'

Finn grasped the leather handles of the first bag, levering it up to the level of the helicopter floor. Jenessa leaned forward to take it from him, and as he gave a final heave saw him gasp with pain, his features contorted. 'Are you okay?' she asked in quick concern.

He shoved the pack toward her, not meeting her eyes. 'Yeah... out of shape, that's all.'

He didn't look like a man who was out of shape. But she swallowed any other questions because Wally had begun his pre-flight check and they were already late. Carefully she leaned her cherrywood paddle against the pile of packs and jumped down to the ground. 'That's it—let's go.'

Ryan gave her a light punch on the arm and said gruffly, 'Stay away from souse holes, won't ya?'

Jenessa grinned at him. 'Finish the wallpapering while I'm gone.'

She climbed into the back seat and strapped herself in. As Finn eased himself into the passenger seat, twisting his body in the confined space, another spasm of pain tightened his features. If there was something wrong, she thought grimly, he should have told her. She had first-aid training, but there were no doctors where they were going.

Within minutes they lifted off the ground. As the houses diminished beneath them, she adjusted her headset, amused to hear Wally, as much as he was capable of being deferential, deferring to Finn. Whatever Finn did, it must be big league; helicopters, as well she knew, didn't come cheap and helicopter pilots were notorious for their independence. Then she saw Finn unfold his map. 'Can you fly me over this island, Wally?' he asked. 'There should be an old house on it.'

'Sure thing,' Wally said easily. 'The boss told me to take you wherever you wanted to go.'

Jenessa didn't want to fly over the Hilchey land. She had counted on entering it gradually, adjusting day by day to the landscape she loved. Biting her lip, she watched as the town and the grey ribbon of highway dropped away behind them, to be replaced by the dense green of trees and the paler green of the barrens. Within half an hour they had reached Caribou Lodge, its tall windows bouncing back the sun's glare. Wally followed the twisting course of the river south, pointing out the lakes and ponds to Finn. Her eyes glued to the window, Jenessa saw the white patch of Osprey Falls and the meandering trail of Beothuck Brook with its groves of silver-trunked birches. She had caught her first trout in that brook, and had swum with her father in the pool below the falls, the cold water making her skin tingle... Juniper Lake, Little Bog Pond, Cranberry Lake—one by one they slipped below her. Then, in the distance, the cove on Spruce Pond glittered in the sunlight.

She was too far away to pick out the cabin where she had grown up. To her horror her eyes crowded with tears, blurring the landscape into an impressionistic haze of blues and greens.

Finn turned in his seat. 'Jenessa, do you—what's wrong?'

Wally, too, glanced over his shoulder. Wishing both of them a thousand miles away, swiping away the tear that had trickled down her cheek, she choked, 'Nothing.'

Finn's eyes bored into hers. He knew she was lying. But he'd wait for an explanation, she thought uneasily.

Wait as a hunter must wait. He said brusquely, 'Can you pick out the house if we go over it?'

She nodded, fighting back emotions as keenly felt now as they had been when she was thirteen. She'd been a fool to agree to this, an utter fool.

Blinking hard, she saw below her the shores of the unimaginatively named Middle Lake, with its egg-shaped island in the dead center of the lake. As Wally brought the helicopter lower and the trees took on individual shapes and sizes, the angled line of a roof high on the cliffs at one end of the island sprang into view. 'There,' she said. 'You can even see the remains of the wharf among the rocks.'

'No place to land,' Wally said cheerfully. 'Too bad.'

Finn said nothing. He, like Jenessa, was staring at the ground, his jaw set, his face empty of expression.

Wally brought the helicopter round, heading north back toward the lodge. Jenessa gazed down at her linked hands in her lap, breathing deeply to settle her nerves. With a bit of luck Finn wouldn't remember she'd been crying; and Mac had never been overly observant—he wouldn't notice any traces of tears on her cheeks.

Wally landed the helicopter with delicate precision in the middle of the clipped grass to the left of the lodge and pulled off his headset. 'Keep your heads low,' he yelled. 'We'll unload the gear in a few minutes.'

Jenessa slid to the ground, ducking until she was beyond the reach of the rotors. As Finn joined her, Mac came striding across the grass to meet them. His charm, she noticed, was very much in evidence. 'Jenessa,' he said, 'how nice to see you again. And you must be Finn Marston. Lloyd MacDonald, better known as Mac.'

The wind from the blades was disarranging his wavy blond hair. Smoothing it back, speaking exclusively to

Finn, he went on, 'Let me show you to your room and I'll look after your gear later. Dinner's not until eight, to give the fishermen the chance to get back, so you'll have lots of time for a drink at the bar first. I hope you'll enjoy your stay with us.'

'Where's Jenessa staying?' Finn said abruptly.

For a moment something less pleasant than charm hardened Mac's pale blue eyes. Then he said heartily, 'There's a cabin for the guides in the back of the lodge. She will, of course, join us for dinner.'

Finn smiled at her. 'Drinks are on me,' he said. 'See you later.'

What Finn was saying, of course, was that she also was joining them at the bar, whether Mac liked it or not. 'I think we should get out in the canoe for an hour before dinner, Finn,' she said. 'There's not much wind and it'll give us a head start for tomorrow. Why don't you meet me at the dock in ten or fifteen minutes?'

If he had staked his claim, she was now staking hers: I'm your guide; what I say goes. Mac said bluffly, 'Give the guy a break, Jenessa; lots of time for that tomorrow.'

'Fifteen minutes?' Jenessa repeated, her eyes as green as the grass on which she was standing.

'Yes, ma'am,' said Finn, and winked at her.

She kept her face straight with an effort and headed back to the helicopter to unload it and say goodbye to Wally. Within fifteen minutes the helicopter had gone and she had the paddles and life-jackets neatly lined up on the dock, where a dark green cedar canoe was moored. The lake sparkled in the sun, the wind was minimal and the dock was out of sight of the lodge, which meant they could practice unobserved.

Finn arrived precisely on time, his faded jeans and close-fitting T-shirt far from new; his muscles, Jenessa thought unwillingly, were truly impressive. She said, 'We'll work for an hour—that'll still give you time for a drink.'

As if she hadn't spoken, Finn asked, 'Why were you crying in the helicopter?'

Her lips compressed. 'For personal reasons that are nothing to do with you.'

'You might as well tell me now as later.'

'I'm not going to tell you at all,' she retorted. 'We'll try out the basic strokes on the dock, then we'll practice getting in and out of the canoe.'

'You'll tell me,' he repeated with soft menace. Then he glanced down at the canoe. 'The two of us and all our gear are supposed to fit in that? It looks as if it'd tip over if you sneezed.'

'I promise it won't. But tomorrow or the next day we'll tip it on purpose and do some rescue techniques. Try this paddle; I think it's long enough for you.'

She knelt at the edge of the dock, showing him the grip and the basic power stroke, all her movements unhurried and seemingly effortless. But when he took the first slice through the water with his paddle, she saw him flinch.

'Is there something wrong, Finn?' As he shook his head and took a second stroke, she persisted, 'I noticed the same thing when you were loading the food into the helicopter.'

'Don't fuss, Jenessa,' he said tersely. 'I collided with a winch a couple of weeks ago and tore some muscles. It's nothing.'

'Now you tell me,' she responded with pardonable sharpness. 'Once we set out we might be paddling ten hours a day—if you're injured, I have to know about it.'

'On a scale of one to ten, it's a three,' he replied. 'Am I doing this right?'

She stood up. 'Show me,' she ordered.

Finn put down the paddle and got to his feet. 'We might as well get one thing straight right now,' he rasped. 'A good leader doesn't abuse his—or her—authority.' Then he peeled off his T-shirt, holding it in one hand.

Jenessa gave a gasp of horror. A livid bruise stretched the length of his ribcage. A big patch of skin that had been scraped from his belly was starting to heal over; it did not look pretty. Another, older scar dipped beneath the waistband of his jeans.

'What happened there?' she whispered.

'A chemical burn. Two years ago.'

Dark hair funnelled down his chest to his navel; as he lifted one hand to rake back his hair, the muscles moved smoothly under his skin. She dragged her eyes away and said the first thing that came into her mind. 'Do you work on the oil rigs?'

'In a manner of speaking. I run a company that fights blowouts on wells. Oil and gas.' He shrugged. 'It's hazardous work and sometimes you get hurt.'

'Is that why you look so exhausted?' she said bluntly.

'You see too much, Jenessa.' He pulled the T-shirt over his head. 'Look, we came here so you could teach me one end of a canoe from the other—why don't we get on with it? If there's one thing I've learned in the last ten years, it's how far I can push myself. Believe me, paddling for ten hours is going to be a breeze.'

The words came out without conscious intention. 'I think you push yourself too far. And too hard.'

'When I want your opinion I'll ask for it,' Finn said unpleasantly. 'Stick to canoeing, why don't you?'

I'm never rude to clients, Jenessa thought, gritting her teeth. 'Keep the paddle vertical,' she said. 'Plant it a comfortable distance ahead of you and end the stroke just past your hip; that way you get the most power with the least effort. This is how you feather the paddle when you bring it forward again—it cuts down on wind resistance.'

She was a good teacher; she led him patiently and thoroughly through the basic strokes, encouraged by his quick grasp of the essentials and his retentive memory. Before they got in the canoe, she said with a perfectly straight face, 'We'll start out with you in the bow and me in the stern. You're responsible for keeping an eye out for rocks and deadheads, but as stern paddler I'm in command... got that?'

He laughed outright. 'Why do I keep getting the feeling the dice are loaded?'

'I'd instantly abdicate command were we on an oil rig,' she bantered, entranced by how carefree he looked when he laughed.

For a moment Finn looked around him at the gently waving boughs of the junipers that overhung the ruffled blue of the lake; the only sound was the slap of tiny waves against the dock. 'I can't imagine two worlds more different,' he said.

'Which one do you prefer?' Jenessa asked, and found herself holding her breath for the answer.

But his face had closed against her. 'Ask me that in another week... Now, how do I get into this canoe without dumping both of us in the drink?'

They paddled for half an hour, then docked the canoe. 'You've earned a visit to the bar; you're doing fine,' Jenessa said. 'I'll see you later.'

'Aren't you coming?' he rapped.

'I've got work to do—you're paying me a hundred dollars a day, Finn.'

'I'll help carry your gear to the guide cabin.'

She grimaced. 'I'm not going to sleep there—I'll pitch a tent by the lake. Mac's guides have the tendency to be party animals.'

'There are empty rooms in the lodge,' Finn said, frowning.

'You're the guest, I'm the employee—Mac likes to keep that distinction.'

'You'll join me at the bar, Jenessa—that's an order from your employer.'

She rolled her eyes heavenward. 'Half an hour. Don't drink all the whiskey.'

Thirty-five minutes later she walked into the bar. She loved its varnished pine beams and tall windows and hated its array of stuffed bears, game birds and glassy-eyed caribou that dated from Mac's taxidermy days. One of the other guests, a silver-haired French count who was an avid fisherman, remembered her from two years ago; he lifted her hand to his lips and said with a courtly bow, 'How delightful to see you again, my dear—never have I caught a salmon the equal of the one you led me to on the Exploits River. And your hair...charming.' He turned to Finn. 'It gives her the look of a choirboy, pure and untouched—wouldn't you agree?'

'You're an incurable romantic,' Jenessa teased.

'No, he isn't,' Finn said smoothly. 'The man's a realist.'

'I wouldn't call her untouched,' Mac said with a ferocious smile at his former guide. 'Rum and Coke, Jen?'

Conquering a strong urge to plant her foot square on Mac's moccasined toe, Jenessa said, 'I've graduated to something more sophisticated since you knew me, Mac—

I'll have a Glenfiddich, please,' and all the while was aware of Finn following every nuance of this interchange. Then three other guests and two more guides came in, one of whom had made a pass at her the one and only time she had stayed in the guide cabin, the other of whom she liked very much. She contrived to sit with him at dinner and at nine-thirty, when Finn was bent over a map with two of the other guests, headed for her tent.

For some reason Ryan had packed a three-person tent; while it meant she would have to carry the extra weight at portages, it also meant she had lots of room. She went to sleep to the wailing of a loon on the far side of the lake and woke at dawn to a light rain.

The next two days went by very quickly as she coached Finn in bow and stern strokes and the crucial effects of wind. He learned fast. He was also strong and seemingly tireless despite his injury; but the hours they spent outdoors didn't remove the shadows from beneath his eyes or the lines etched in his forehead. Somehow in the last few years, Jenessa was more and more convinced, Finn Marston had lost the ability to relax. He'd forgotten how to play. How to have fun. Sure, he could laugh at his own ineptness when the canoe went in the opposite direction to that which he had planned; but then he would practice with fierce concentration until he had corrected his mistake. To Finn ineptness meant inefficiency, and that, she thought, he couldn't tolerate.

Always, underlying everything they did, she sensed his impatience to be done with the lessons and to be on their way, an impatience held in check only by his formidable will-power.

Late in the afternoon of the second day, when the clouds had cleared and the sun had warmed the air, she said, 'Okay, we'll do some rescue techniques. But first you should know how to change places. Here we are in the middle of the lake and we want to switch positions. As bow person, you go first. Back up to the middle of the canoe and crouch down. I move forward to the bow; when I'm settled, you move back to the stern. Let's go.'

With the agility that she had come to expect of him, Finn backed up and crouched midships. Holding the gunwales and keeping her weight low, Jenessa stepped forward. But Finn was a big man. She inched round him, balancing her feet on either side of his hips, her hands resting on his broad shoulders. She felt him tense, the muscles hardening beneath her fingers. She said lightly, 'It's all right, I promise we're not going to capsize,' then crawled forward to the cane seat at the bow.

Finn straightened, rubbing at the back of his neck. 'You thought I was afraid of falling in just then? That's a joke.'

She frowned. 'Why else were you so tense?'

'For God's sake, grow up, Jenessa,' he said roughly and edged back to the stern seat.

It was not the first time in the last two days that Jenessa had sensed an anger toward her whose source had eluded her. Sex, she now thought in a flash of insight. He's talking about sex. He doesn't like it that I'm oblivious to him as a man. That's why he didn't like me touching him just then. That's why he told me to grow up.

She hated both his anger and the reason for it—because he was telling her—as both Ruth and Ryan had also told her—that she was a misfit. Out of touch with her sexuality.

It was a message she didn't need to hear again.

Especially from Finn Marston.

CHAPTER FIVE

KEEPING her thoughts to herself, Jenessa repeated the maneuver of changing seats in the canoe, hunching down low in the bilge. As Finn edged round her, he managed not to touch her at all. Good for you, she thought, and said coldly, 'We'll tip the canoe next and I'll show you how we'd get it back to shore.'

She stood up, balancing on the gunwales, a slim figure in shorts that bared her long legs, and began bouncing the canoe from side to side. Finn used the wrong brace stroke and with a greedy gurgle lakewater rushed into the canoe. He lost his balance and in a great splash went under. Jenessa slipped easily into the water and was waiting for him when he surfaced, his wet hair slicked to his skull. He shook himself like a dog and took a couple of powerful crawl strokes toward her. 'You enjoyed doing that, didn't you?'

'Thought it might cool your temper,' Jenessa said. 'Rule one—hold on to the canoe and check that your partner's okay.'

He grabbed the keel, his blue eyes blazing with an emotion she couldn't have deciphered, and snarled, 'For someone who knows one hell of a lot of men, you seem to be totally unaware of the male sex.'

She should have proceeded to rule two. 'Don't be silly,' she flared, 'I work with men all the time; of course I'm aware of them.'

'Have you ever gone to bed with any of them? Apart from Mac, that is.'

Breaking her own rule, Jenessa let go of the canoe and took a swift stroke away from him. 'That's none of your business.'

'Until I met Mac, I'd have staked a year's salary that you were a virgin.'

Insulted, enraged and, worst of all, hurt, Jenessa cried, 'I don't see why my virginity or lack of it should concern you in the least!'

The water swirling round his chest, Finn closed the distance between them. 'You don't even know that I'm a man!'

Fear added itself to all the other emotions churning in her breast. 'Of course I do. Up until five minutes ago I would have said I was even beginning to like you.'

Finn's jaw suddenly dropped. He said blankly, 'You're into women—I never thought of that.'

It took a moment for his meaning to penetrate. So angry that she forgot to tread water, Jenessa swallowed a mouthful of the lake and sputtered, 'I am not!' Abandoning truth along with the canoe, she added, 'Just ask Mac.'

'So you *were* lovers...he's not worth your little finger.'

'How nice that I'm confirming your lack of respect for the female half of humanity,' she raged, and then saw, to her horror, that while they had been arguing they had also been drifting closer to shore. The count, his silver hair gleaming, his fishing-rod in one hand, was striding along the shoreline.

Sound traveled over water and the count had an excellent grasp of English. 'We have an audience,' Jenessa announced with fatalistic calm.

Finn said an unprintable word under his breath. 'At least out in the wilderness we'll be able to fight without the whole world participating.'

Biting off her words, she said, 'If you hired me thinking I'd spend the next two weeks falling all over you, you've got the wrong woman. I'm not the slightest bit interested in you sexually; have you got that straight?'

'You think I need you telling me that? I'm not totally obtuse, Jenessa Reed.'

He was shouting again. The count tactfully flailed at some alder branches and then splashed through the shallows in his hipwaders. If Finn and I haven't already scared away every trout within five miles, Jenessa thought with a twinge of hysterical laughter, the count's just finished off the job himself. 'Let's right this gol-darned canoe and call it a day,' she snapped.

'Fine with me.'

They turned the canoe over, swam it to shore and dumped out the water, the silence between them broken only by some brief orders from Jenessa. Then they paddled back to the dock. Jenessa climbed out and moored the canoe. I'm never rude to clients, she thought despairingly, and said with a valiant, if not particularly sincere attempt at politeness, 'We'll leave tomorrow morning after breakfast. Have your gear all in one backpack and ready to go. I'll see you at dinner.'

Finn unzippered his wet life-jacket. 'The sooner we go, the sooner we'll get back,' he grated, turned on his heel and headed for the lodge.

She felt ridiculously like crying. She trailed back to her tent, shucked off her wet clothes and hung them out to dry, and looked at her watch. Two hours until dinner. She shouldn't be so efficient; she had absolutely nothing to do for that two hours.

She didn't know why she was so upset. It certainly wasn't the first time sex had caused problems in her job, and she was normally adept at dealing with these problems. But at some unacknowledged level from the moment she had first seen him, exhausted and impatient at the airport terminal, she had thought Finn Marston would be different.

She had been wrong.

She looked at her watch again. Three minutes had passed.

She could have a hot shower and wash her hair; it would be her last shower in two weeks. But the bathrooms were located in the lodge and she didn't want to bump into Finn.

She could walk to the headwaters of the lake and sit and watch the rapids.

She stood up with sudden energy. She knew what she was going to do; she was going to borrow Mac's white-water canoe and run the rapids. That would take her mind off Finn.

By sheer good luck Mac was outside with one of the guests and made no objection to her borrowing the canoe. She took it from the boathouse, paddled to the head of the lake, and portaged it along the trail that followed the river's edge. There had been a fair amount of rain in August; periodically she leaned the canoe against a tree and checked out her course.

Half an hour later Jenessa launched the canoe in the deep pool at the head of the rapids. The roar and hiss of tons of water surging between the rocks filled her ears, and she felt her mouth dry and her heart begin to pound. Braced against the seat, her knees spread wide, she angled the canoe across the river, seeking out the V-shaped channel that indicated a break in the rocks, then steering towards it. The canoe gathered speed and plunged through the gap, the bow cutting into the standing waves so that spray dashed against her bare arms. With a wild whoop of exhilaration she thrust her paddle into the water in a high brace and forgot about everything but the seething whitewater of which she and the canoe were so integral a part.

Twice on the way down she steered into eddies, patches of calm water below the rocks, where she could take a breath and read the rapids to plan her course. The second eddy was just above the final, and worst, stretch of the river. Squinting, she saw that there was only one break in the ledge fifty feet away. Some hard draws would take her there, and the haystacks of white foam below the ledge were no problem. The things to avoid were the souse holes to her left. Ryan had taught her a healthy respect for souse holes.

Totally concentrated on what she was doing, she didn't see the tall figure of a man crouched on a granite boulder at the foot of the rapids, tension in every inch of his stance. Settling herself more deeply in the canoe, she stroked out into the current, backpaddling to keep her speed under control above the long ledge of jagged rocks. Then the channel was right in front of her. With another whoop of excitement she steered through it. The bow of the canoe curvetted skywards and foam drenched her thighs.

Sculling, prying, bracing, using all the skills at her command, her body fluid and perfectly balanced, Jenessa rode the torrential waters, the canoe bucking like a wild pony one moment, sliding sleekly through the dark channels between the waves the next. Then, all too soon, the open pool at the base of the rapids was ahead of her. With a wide sweep she brought the canoe round to shore, gazing back the way she had come, and let out a peal of exultant laughter.

From the corner of her eye she caught a flicker of movement on the land. She swung her head round. A man was leaping down the slope to the river, gripping the boulders with strong fingers as he went, his long legs as agile as a caribou's. Finn. He had been watching her.

He reached the river's edge, shucked off his deck shoes and waded into the bubble-flecked water, waves rippling from his thighs. Jenessa's canoe was only fifteen feet from shore. His gaze was trained on her face, on her flushed cheeks and parted lips, where exhilaration lingered as vivid as sunlight. Leaning forward, he grabbed the prow of the canoe.

Mac's canoe was designed for maximum maneuverability; as it tipped sideways Jenessa yelped, 'If you dump me in the river after I made it all the way down those rapids, Finn Marston, I'll never speak to you again!'

Automatically he righted it, gripping it on either side of the bow. His eyes burning into hers, he said hoarsely, 'You and I are alike—we're both risk-takers, Jenessa! You need that rush of adrenaline just as I do. Don't you understand? I've just seen a side of you I've never seen before. Like calls to like, Jenessa.'

She swallowed hard, her heartbeat thudding in her ears as only moments ago the roar of water had deafened her. With total truth she said, 'Sometimes risk is a place I run away to. When everything else gets too much.'

Her reply was plainly not what Finn had expected. Frowning, he asked, 'What were you running from?'

'Who, not what. You, of course.'

He pulled the canoe closer to shore under the dappled shadows of the maples that lined the river. His frown deepening, he said, more to himself than to her, 'Maybe that's why I'm here...because I'm trying to stop running.'

Then, before she could guess his intention, he planted his feet among the rocks, took her under the armpits and lifted her from the canoe. Weightless in mid-air, utterly astonished, Jenessa made an instinctive move to kick out and struggle. But just in time she remembered his scarred belly and bruised ribs and let herself hang limp in his arms. As he put her down at the very edge of the water and reached for the rope on the canoe, she choked, 'Cut out the he-man stuff!'

He hauled the canoe up on the shore and turned back to her. His movements swift and very sure of themselves, he unzipped her life-jacket, pulled it off and tossed it on the ground. Then he reached out for her, his arms hard around her waist.

He was far more dangerous than any river, she thought dazedly. For this time his intention was quite clear: he was going to kiss her.

As if it were happening to someone else, she watched him bend his head, and felt the pressure of his mouth on hers. His lips were warm against her spray-damp skin; they moved from her mouth to caress her cheek and the taut line of her jaw.

Shock and surprise had held Jenessa rigid; in a surge of panic she pushed him away. One kiss from Finn Marston had crossed a barrier that she'd wanted inviolate. Had needed inviolate. She gasped, 'Don't, Finn—please don't. You're changing everything and I don't want that.'

His eyes reflecting the churning blue-black of the river, Finn said, 'I watched you come down those rapids. You can't fool me—you don't play it safe any more than I do.'

'There are some risks I choose not to take. Getting involved with you is one of them!'

She wasn't even sure he'd heard her. He said urgently, 'Do you know what you looked like when I waded out to you? You looked like a woman who's just made love... all night long, slowly and thoroughly and with enormous pleasure.'

The wind rustled among the leaves, stroking Jenessa's damp body with its cool fingers. Finn's words made her deeply afraid, more afraid than she'd been of anything or anyone since she was sixteen. Shivering, she felt more strongly than ever before the huge abyss that seemed to stretch between her and other people. She knew the technicalities of how men and women made love; of course she did. Yet none of Mac's kisses or rough fumblings with her clothes had tempted her to take the plunge into those particular waters.

The excitement of running the rapids, the total involvement of body and mind, the sensation of being poised on the brink of danger and the sheer thrill of the descent—sex couldn't be like that. It wasn't possible.

'Finn,' she said tightly, 'tomorrow we're heading out for two weeks, just the two of us. Alone. I have to know you're not going to do this kind of thing to me. It'll be impossible for me to do my job if you're going to be harassing me all the time.'

'Harassing you?' he repeated in a strange voice. 'That's how you saw that kiss—as harassment?'

She looked him full in the face and what she saw there almost made her cry out with distress. His features were a battleground where frustration and that all-encompassing exhaustion fought for supremacy with something she would have sworn was pain; and only will-power tamped each of these emotions down. He let his hands fall from her waist and said evenly, 'You'd better go and get changed; you're cold.'

'I'm sorry, I know I'm not like other women—but that's the way I am!'

'Leave it, Jenessa.'

In a low voice she said, 'There are some waters I have no idea how to navigate and no desire to explore.'

'You'll be quite safe with me,' Finn said with a formal precision that was as cold as ice. 'I promise you that... I'll see you at dinner.'

His wet bush pants clinging to his thighs, he started up the slope among the granite boulders. Jenessa lifted the canoe back into the river and climbed in. With long, steady strokes she headed for the lake.

She had Finn's promise that he wouldn't touch her again.

He was, she would swear, a man of his word.

No matter what it cost him.

Jenessa showered before dinner, dried her clothes in the generator-powered machine, and at the count's insistence joined him, Mac and Finn for dinner. If she was quieter than usual, no one seemed to notice. As soon as the meal was over, she went to the kitchen to check on the food for the trip. It was dark when she finally headed for her tent.

She walked soft-footed down the trail through the alders to her campsite. Ten feet from the tent she stopped in her tracks. The smell of cigarette smoke drifted to her nostrils and a tiny point of orange light glowed in the blackness. 'Is that you, Mac?' she said sharply.

The dark bulk of a man's body moved toward her. 'Yeah, it's me. Took your time getting back... were you fooling around with Marston again?'

'No,' she said drily, 'I wasn't. What do you want?'

Mac came closer; in the light from his cigarette his eyes gaped like the black holes in a mask. 'Thought you and I should have a little chat before you headed out,' he said. 'You know why Marston wants to look over the Hilchey land, don't you?'

Jenessa shoved her hands in the pockets of her bush pants, suddenly aware that she was frightened of what she might hear. 'Mac, it's late and I'm tired. This'll keep until we get back.'

'Oh, I don't think so. I don't think you'd thank me if I let you take off into the woods with Finn Marston without telling you just who he is.'

Mac was playing her as a fisherman played the fish he wanted to hook. Refusing to bite, she said, 'I know who he is. He runs a business that caps oil-well blow-outs—he flew here from Indonesia.'

'That's true enough, I guess. But there's a lot more to him than that, Jen.'

Her throat was dry, as if once again she were poised at the head of the rapids. 'So why don't you tell me, Mac? Tell me and get it over with.'

'Finn Marston owns Hilchey's land. He inherited it.'

Her voice a thin thread in the darkness, she repeated, 'Owns it? He can't!'

'I told you—he inherited it. All four thousand acres of it. Including the land that used to be your dad's.'

The land that had been wrested from her father, that had caused his death, now belonged to Finn. Feeling as though the ground had shifted under her feet, Jenessa croaked, 'I don't believe you! Why would Finn have inherited it?'

'He's Hilchey's grandson.'

Her brain scrambling for the solidity of facts, she cried, 'He can't be! George Hilchey's daughter was married to a man called Wilfred Ellis—so his grandson's last name would be Ellis. Not Marston.'

'Yeah, I figured that one out, too. So I checked up on him before he got here. Seems that at the age of eighteen Finn Ellis legally changed his last name to Marston. Hilchey's wife Amy—who by all accounts was a half-decent old biddy, as different from her husband as she could be—her maiden name was Marston.'

Her head reeling, Jenessa repeated numbly, 'Finn is George Hilchey's grandson... so that's why he wants to go to the old summer house.'

Mac dropped his cigarette butt and ground it into the dirt. Her eyes were accustomed to the darkness now; she saw him shrug. 'The summer house is where his mother committed suicide... they tried to hush that up, but my dad was the caretaker there that summer, and he told me what happened. Shot herself with one of her father's hunting guns.'

It was an old story, something that had happened when Jenessa was only seven, but Mac's callous recital still had the power to make her wince. 'So Marion Ellis was Finn's mother,' she whispered.

'That's right. Kind of a strange woman, according to my dad—not what you'd call happy. Never had much use for her son, by all reports.'

'He must have changed his name soon after she killed herself.'

'Don't you go feeling sorry for him,' Mac said. 'I bet he inherited a whole lot more than a chunk of central Newfoundland— he's not hurting. Not one bit.'

Wasn't he? Jenessa wasn't so sure. She closed her eyes, the inner darkness under her lids echoing the outer. The little cove where she had grown up, the birch meadows where the moose lay down to rest, the tumbling waters of the brook and the sandy beach where she had learned to swim—Finn owned them all. He had inherited what his grandfather had stolen.

'I hated George Hilchey for years,' she said, speaking more to herself than to Mac. 'Ryan made me stop—said it was eating me up.'

'Then I wouldn't advise you to get too friendly with his grandson,' Mac said.

She stared at him, belatedly trying to think. 'Is that why you told me all this? To protect me?'

His teeth flashed white in the gloom. 'Not exactly,' he said. 'Why should I bother protecting you? No, I want to buy the land from him. He'll be getting offers from the logging companies and from mining outfits too, more than likely. But I want it—it adjoins my land and it'd give me a monopoly on this whole area. Some of the best hunting and fishing in the province. I'd be laughing.'

With another ugly jolt in her chest Jenessa said, 'He's going to *sell* it?'

'Sure he is—he's got no interest in living in the middle of Newfoundland; he can't run his business from here. What else will he do with it but sell it? It's no good to him.'

The words battered at her composure. 'So what's that got to do with me?'

'I know how you feel about conservation. Tell him that if he sells to logging or mining interests they'll destroy the whole area. Whereas I'd leave it be. You'd like that, wouldn't you?'

'You want me to persuade Finn Marston to sell Hilchey's land to you?' She gave a short, unamused laugh. 'You don't know him very well. No one could persuade him to do anything he didn't already want to do.'

'Try, Jen. I can get you lots of work here in the next few years if I expand into that property.'

'A little bribery?' she said wryly. Suddenly attacked by a desperate need to be alone, she said, 'I can't promise anything, Mac, you must see that.'

He stepped closer, his smoke-laden breath wafting her cheek, his fingers closing hard around her arm. 'Try, Jen,' he repeated. 'Because if I can get you jobs I can take them away just as easily. If I put my mind to it I could go a long way to wrecking your reputation as a guide.'

It was the second time in less than a week that this particular threat had been directed at her. This time she had her answer ready. 'I'd sue you for slander.'

He said smoothly, his fingers digging into her arm, 'I didn't really want Marston coming here—wanted him to sell me the land sight unseen. But now that he's here I might as well use you to get to him. It's to everyone's advantage that he sell to me; you're smart enough to figure that one out. Work on it, won't you?'

One final squeeze of his fingers and Mac released her arm. Jenessa stood very still, listening to the snap of twigs and the small rustlings of the alder leaves as he walked away from her, back to the lodge. She was alone, as only moments ago she had craved to be.

She would have given every penny that Finn was going to pay her in the next two weeks to be home at Ryan's, making him coffee, listening to him grumble about the exorbitant price of wallpaper and jade-green paint.

How was she going to face Finn tomorrow?

The face that she had seen as handsome, masculine, rough-hewn she now saw as ruthless. No one got to be the boss of a mutli-million-dollar company by being benevolent and altruistic. He had inherited more than land from his grandfather, she thought sickly. He had inherited character, a way of life that applauded the acquiring of wealth and turned a blind eye on the way in which it was acquired.

Like father, like son... substitute grandfather and grandson, and she had the relationship between George Hilchey and Finn Marston. Birds of a feather, a chip off the old block, tarred with the same brush—the clinchés tumbled through her tired brain.

She had to spend the next two weeks with Finn. Guiding him through land that she loved and that he would sell to the highest bidder. Land that meant nothing to him.

How would she bear it?

CHAPTER SIX

JENESSA would have sworn she heard every wave that rippled on the shore throughout the night, every wail of the loons on the lake, every rustle in the undergrowth around her tent. Mac's disclosures, motivated, she knew, entirely by self-interest, had thrust her back into a past she had thought she was finished with. In the darkness of her tent she wept for her father, who from his own weaknesses and the schemings of a rich man had lost everything he loved; and wept, too, for the young girl whose life had been taken over by authorities who, for all their good intentions, had had no understanding of her at all.

The one thing she didn't do was sleep. For the other face that hung in front of her eyes the whole night through was Finn's. The shock of discovering he was George Hilchey's grandson had made her realize how deeply he had infiltrated her defenses in only four short days. His impatience, his exhaustion, his rare flashes of humor, all the contrasts of a man not easily read, had interested her from the very beginning. Fascinated her, she thought honestly, staring at the stars through the mosquito netting. He was unlike anyone else she had ever met.

If she were really honest, she would admit that she had cherished the hope that she and the wilderness through which she would guide him would nourish him in some way. Heal him.

He wasn't heading into the wilderness for healing. He was assessing what price he could get for land that was of no other value to him.

As the slow hours passed she could find it in her to be grateful to Mac. She was forewarned. She knew Finn's motive. She could now retreat inside herself, protect herself from any involvement with a man who could only bring her grief.

At the first light of dawn she slipped out of her tent in her trim green swimsuit and ran headlong into the lake. The water struck cool on her skin. Plunging beneath the surface, she swam in strong strokes away from the shore, relishing the pull of her muscles and the slide of water along her body, feeling the first easing of a tension she had carried ever since she had seen Mac waiting for her outside the tent last night.

Turning back, she dived beneath the water, the smooth curve of her back and the pale gleam of her legs disappearing below the surface. She swam until her lungs craved oxygen, burst upwards, seized a huge gulp of air and dived again. So she was only a few feet from the shore when her feet touched bottom and she stood, panting and swiping at the water that streamed down her face. Only then did she open her eyes.

With a strange sense of *déjà vu* she saw that Finn was balanced on the rocks at the edge of the lake, waiting for her. Last night, Mac. This morning, Finn. Anger ripped through her, shocking her with its intensity. Her feet seeking purchase among the smooth rocks, she waded toward him, water splashing round her ankles. She forgot that he was her employer, forgot that she was clad only in a swimsuit; in a clipped voice she said, 'What do *you* want?'

He waited until she was level with him. Then he seized her by the elbow. His touch turned Jenessa's anger into red-hot rage. 'Let go of me!'

'No—not until you've heard me out.'

Her eyes widened, for he sounded—and, she realized rather tardily, looked—every bit as angry as she. What right did he have to be angry? 'Then make it fast,' she spat; 'I've got work to do.'

'Oh, it won't take long. Why did you lie to me, Jenessa? All that fancy talk yesterday about waters you didn't know how to navigate and weren't willing to explore—and then last night you invite Mac to your tent. You and he have been lovers all along, haven't you?'

His face was scoured with contempt; the grip of his fingers was cruelly strong. That he also looked as if he had slept as little as she she ignored. It was as if George Hilchey stood in front of her, ruthless George Hilchey, believing the worst of everyone, using brute force to crush those who opposed him. She said with icy clarity, 'Go away, Finn. I have nothing to say to you—nothing.'

'That's why you didn't want to sleep in the guides' cabin— Mac couldn't visit you there, could he?'

'You're as wrong as——'

'Why didn't you let him stay all night, Jenessa? Afraid that people might catch on? That your lily-white image might be sullied?'

'You don't listen, do you? I don't have anything to say to you and I don't give a damn what you think of me—think what you like. Just go away and leave me alone!'

'I thought you were different—that's what I thought. I thought you were honest. I even thought—don't laugh, will you?— that you had a quality of innocence I'd never expected to find. I was wrong on all three counts, wasn't I? As wrong as I could be!'

'I've had enough of this,' she stormed. 'You and I are employer and employee. Nothing more. You're paying me a hundred dollars a day to guide for you, and that's what I'll do. But don't expect anything else from me—is that clear?'

He dropped her elbow. 'You think I'd want anything else? I don't take other men's leavings.'

Jenessa should have picked up her towel from the bush where she had draped it, covered herself with it and maintained a dignified silence until he'd left. 'You see everything in terms of sex, don't you?' she said shrewishly. 'But I suppose if you don't respect women that's all they're good for.'

His eyes raked her body up and down. 'Some of them aren't even good for that.'

She flinched, for he had hit her where she was most vulnerable. In her innermost heart she had sometimes wondered if she embodied that word frigid that was bandied about in all the popular magazines; if, for reasons beyond her, she was barred from experiencing the pleasures that other women seemed to take for granted. The articles that spoke so knowingly about sex seemed to be written in a language which excluded her, the participant strangers in another land. She had not once been driven to make love to a man with all the heart-pounding urgency that the writers described so eloquently. And Ruth and Ryan were right: she met dozens of men, far more than the average female. So there must be something wrong with her. She was a misfit. Cold. Useless as a woman. She said flatly, 'Have your gear on the dock before breakfast. We'll leave right after we've eaten.'

But Finn was staring at her arm. In a voice she had never heard him use before, he said, 'Those bruises—Mac did that, didn't he?'

'It's nothing; I bruise easily. Anyway, I'll probably have bruises on my elbow by tomorrow.'

Appalled, Finn dropped his hold on her as if her skin were scalding him. 'I don't know what the hell's the matter with me! I've never behaved like this in my life—yelled at a woman, grabbed her, fought her as if my life depended on the outcome.'

Steeling herself against the naked emotion in his face, for she didn't want him to be anyone other than a ruthless businessman who was paying her salary, Jenessa said, 'I'm really not interested in the way you treat women. I've got work to do—would you please go away?'

He said quietly, 'Mac's not fit to wipe your boots, Jenessa. We both know that. I'll see you later.'

As he walked away, the olive-green of his bush pants and the green of his shirt blended in with the alders; he was soft-footed for so big a man. Jenessa let out her breath in a long sigh. If Finn was behaving atypically, so too was she. Had been ever since she'd met him.

Two weeks was beginning to sound like forever.

The first day seemed like forever to Jenessa. Before she and Finn left the dock, she took out her maps and showed him the route she had plotted, a U-shaped route where they would travel via a chain of lakes and portages to the summer house, and use the river as much as possible on their return, when its current would be with them. Then they set out. They paddled hard all morning, ate lunch with a minimum of conversation and fought a headwind all afternoon. At four the rain that had been threatening all day started to patter on the lake.

Two hours later Jenessa yelled forward to the man in the bow, 'See that next promontory? That's where we'll camp.'

The landing was tricky, because of rocks. But Finn, she had to admit, had absorbed everything she'd taught him, and handled himself with considerable panache. Once they'd disembarked, Jenessa untied the gear and passed it up to him, her feet digging for purchase in the loose shale. Then they lifted the cedar canoe up the bank, turning it bottom up and tucking the life-jackets and paddles underneath.

The promontory was graced by a stand of white pines, the ground soft with fallen needles. She said crisply, 'We'll pitch the tents in that flat area between the two tallest trees. Maybe you could help me put the tarp up first; that'll protect us from the rain.'

The tarp, which was rolled on the very top of her backpack, was heavy but worth every ounce of its weight. Within five minutes they had it strung from the pine branches; it was large enough to protect two tents from the rain, as well the gear and the cooking fire. 'Tents next,' Jenessa said. 'Can you pitch your own?'

'Sure. Where is it?'

'In the very bottom of your pack—you can get at it with that lower zipper.'

He looked at her quizzically. 'I've got a sleeping-bag and a pad in the bottom of my pack. But no tent. I figured you had both of them.'

'It must be there,' she said with barely disguised impatience. 'In a blue bag—it rolls up very small; you probably didn't realize it was a tent.'

'Jenessa, I took everything out of the pack this morning so I'd know where things were. No tent.'

He wasn't joking; he was telling the truth. Her stomach a cold knot, she muttered, 'Ryan—I'll have his hide for this! He looked after the gear and I didn't bother checking.' Her eyes widened. 'That's why he packed the three-person tent for me...this must be his idea of a joke.'

Finn stated the obvious. 'You don't find it funny.'

'I *never* share a tent with my clients.'

'I'll sleep on the ground under the tarp.'

'The ground's wet and the wind's probably not going to let up until dawn—you'd get soaked,' she said with furious emphasis. 'One thing you can't afford to do on a long trip is get your sleeping-bag wet.'

'I'm not going to fall on you in the night, Jenessa,' he said curtly.

'This isn't about sex, it's about privacy,' she responded equally curtly. 'When I'm with other people for one and two weeks at a stretch, I need time by myself.'

His dark head brushing the orange tarp, Finn drawled, 'Well, I guess you're stuck with me. Do you really think Ryan did this on purpose?'

Too upset to be discreet, she said bitterly, 'Oh, yes. He liked you, I could tell. And he thinks I'm turning into an old maid. Time I settled down and produced a crop of babies.'

'He certainly misconstrued the dynamics between you and me... How old *are* you?'

'Twenty-six next month.'

'Over the hill,' he said.

A small, traitorous part of her wanted to smile in response to the glint in his eyes. Hardening her heart, she said, 'I'll pitch the tent, then I'll get a fire going.'

'I'll pitch the tent. You start the fire.'

'You're paying me to look after you,' she snapped.

'I find that a truly insulting statement.'

He meant every word, she thought, and felt a blush creep up her throat. Refusing to back down, she said, 'Employer and employee, remember? I'm the one who's supposed to do the work.'

'As I seem to repeat with boring frequency, I don't have the faintest idea what's going on here—but, whatever it is, I do know we're in it together. I'll pitch the tent.'

And Jenessa, who had meant to keep Finn firmly in his place, went to gather wood.

For supper she heated the stew that Mac's cook had made, getting out home-made rolls, fresh fruit and date squares to go along with it. As she worked around the fire, she kept reminding herself of Finn's mission; even so, it was extraordinarily difficult to be actively unfriendly with him when she was dodging the leaping flames and enveloped in swirling blue smoke, her nostrils teased by the delicious smell of the stew. She talked very little while they ate and she insisted on cleaning up the dishes; afterwards the two of them hung the bags of food high in a tree away from the campsite to guard against bears. Then she said, 'On long trips I go to bed at dark and get up at dawn—that way you can take advantage of the best paddling early in the morning.'

She was standing by the fire, the flames dancing over her face, the tension in her body all too evident. Finn said, 'You go ahead; I'm going to sit by the fire for a while.'

Were he as ruthless as she had labeled him, he would be accompanying her into the tent and watching her undress. 'Goodnight,' she said awkwardly and ducked under the flap.

She hauled off her boots, leaving them in the little vestibule. Then she saw that Finn had arranged their gear right down the middle of the tent, separating the two sleeping-bags and giving her the maximum privacy possible in so small a space. His action had been at the very least tactful; kind would be a more accurate word. To her horror Jenessa felt tears crowd her eyes.

Confused and unhappy, she pulled off her rain gear and bush pants, folded her sweater for a pillow and snuggled into her sleeping-bag in her T-shirt and underwear. The flames from the campfire were flickering on the blue wall of the tent; she watched as the shadow that was Finn loomed tall, and heard the fire crackle and spit as he put another log on. The shadow disappeared as he sat down again.

She'd never go to sleep. Not when she knew he would soon be lying only a couple of feet away from her.

She closed her eyes, wishing she understood why she felt so miserable—and woke to the high-pitched cry of a Canada jay right outside the tent.

It was daylight. She had slept the night through.

She hadn't even heard Finn come to bed.

Very cautiously Jenessa lifted herself up on one elbow and peered over the edge of her pack. Finn's back was turned to her, his bare shoulders rising and falling with the rhythm of his breathing. He was using his shirt for a pillow. His dark hair was tousled; she found herself staring at the way it curled softly around his ears.

Moving with exquisite care, she pulled on her clothes and crawled out of the tent, managing to do both without disturbing him. As she washed her face and hands in the lake, she gazed around her. The temperature had risen, which meant they'd probably be plagued by flies, the air was dead calm and the purple clouds hanging low over the horizon filled her with disquiet. They were in for some bad weather, unless she was very much mistaken.

She tramped back to the campsite, lowered one of the food bags and got a fire going; when the bacon was sizzling in the pan and water had boiled for coffee, she called Finn's name, rather surprised that he wasn't already up.

He didn't answer; she called him again, turning the strips of bacon at the same time. This time when he didn't respond she crouched down and entered the tent, wondering if he was playing some kind of game with her.

He was lying flat on his stomach, breathing heavily as though he was dreaming, his face buried in his shirt, his arms flung over his head. The sleeping-bag had slipped almost to his waist, baring an expanse of tanned skin; the bruise over his ribs had faded to a jaundiced yellow. His body, she thought with profound unease, was beautifully sculpted. She said loudly, 'It's time to wake up, Finn.'

His head reared up, the muscles bunching in his shoulders. 'Jim,' he gasped, 'did they get him out?'

With a hiss of indrawn breath, for she had never seen such anguish in a man's face, Jenessa said urgently, 'Finn, it's me—Jenessa.'

He shook his head, like a wounded caribou that was unable to flee because its lifeblood was pouring down its flanks. 'Jenessa ...' he muttered.

With the strange sense that he was using her name to haul himself back to reality, she said weakly, 'You must have been dreaming.'

'Yeah ... sorry.' Heaving himself up on one arm, Finn rubbed at his face with his free hand. 'I'll be out in a minute.'

His face had closed against her; she was perceptive enough to see that he hated having exposed himself to her. 'Breakfast's on the go,' she said with false cheer, and backed out of the tent.

The bacon was on the verge of burning; quickly she moved the pan off the flames, her brain whirling. Who was Jim? What had happened to him to bring that look of intolerable pain to Finn's face?

Two things she was sure of: she lacked the courage to ask and Finn wasn't about to tell her.

Using a long stick, her back to the tent, she started toasting a couple of the rolls Mac's cook had baked. With a *frisson* along her spine she heard the rustle of the tent flap as Finn emerged. He strode off down to the lake.

When he came back, carrying his towel and toothbrush, she was dusting the eggs with pepper. 'Smells good,' he remarked.

'It'll be dried food soon enough; we'd better enjoy this while we can...eggs over?'

'Please. Can I make you a coffee?'

'Sure.' Politeness was being used to smother something she hadn't been meant to see, she thought, accepting a mug of coffee from him and passing him his loaded plate. 'Jam and peanut butter on the log there...help yourself.' Breaking her own eggs into the pan, she added, 'I'm worried about the weather. We've got the longest portage of the trip today, and the flies are liable to eat us alive. We'll break camp and head out as soon as we can.'

'I'll do the dishes this morning.'

She was quite sure there was no point in arguing with him. And how could she neatly categorize him as her employer after what she had seen in his face this morning? 'All right,' she said. 'Bury the bacon fat; we carry out all our garbage and the soap's biodegradable.' Giving him the nearest thing to a smile, she finished, 'I'll make sure I dig out the fly dope.'

The Canada jays were back, big grey and white birds attracted by the smell of cooking. Jenessa tossed them some bread scraps. 'They call them whiskeyjacks around here. They get tame pretty fast and they'll steal the food right out of your hand.'

The conversation stayed safely on the subject of wildlife while they ate; within the hour they'd loaded the canoe and were ready to leave. 'Why don't you go in the stern today?' Jenessa suggested. 'We can always change places if a storm comes up.'

He grinned at her. 'You mean I get to steer and give the orders?'

'I've got the map—so I'll be telling you where to go.'

'Maybe,' he said drily, 'that's called equality.'

Out of the blue Jenessa wanted to ask him why he didn't respect women, whether it was because of his mother. She also wanted to ask if he respected her, Jenessa. But she already knew the answer to the latter question: he didn't. She said briefly, 'Let's go.'

They paddled hard for three hours, had a snack on a little sand beach where the mosquitoes descended on them as soon as they landed, and paddled for another couple of hours to the head of the lake. The portage was nearly two miles long, winding uphill through the trees, then crossing a bog that merged into the next lake. 'We'll have to make two trips, but we'll take a break halfway,' Jenessa said. 'Easier on the muscles that way.'

The air was cloyingly warm and very still; the flies were a constant torment. Sweat stung Jenessa's eyes and trickled between her breasts. Her arms ached. Her knees ached. As her boots squelched through the bog on the last leg of the portage, the bow of the canoe balanced on her shoulders, mosquitoes and blackflies rose in hungry hordes. The mosquitoes whined in her ears. The blackflies crept silently into her hair and bit her neck. Grimly she trudged on.

Even the longest of portages had to end. The stones that edged the second lake crunched under her feet. She and Finn swung the canoe down to rest on their thighs, then lowered it to the ground. With a sigh of relief Jenessa untied the bandanna from round her neck and wiped her forehead. 'I wish we had time for a swim,' she said. 'But I want to get to the next campsite before the weather breaks.'

Finn's T-shirt was drenched with sweat, clinging to his chest. 'I'll tell you one thing,' he said, 'you've got stamina, Jenessa. Stamina and strength. A good many men I know couldn't have made that portage.'

She smiled at him spontaneously. 'Thanks,' she said, warmed by the compliment. 'You're no slouch yourself.'

His eyes narrowed. 'Hold still,' he said, reaching out and crushing a blackfly that was biting her neck. His face, unshaven, intent, was very close to hers. As he removed his fingers, she saw with a shiver of superstitious fear that they were stained with her own blood.

Something must have shown in her face. Finn said harshly, 'Let's get out of here.'

The next lake, which had long been a favorite of Jenessa's, was full of small, tree-clad islands and sheltered coves. In one of them they sighted a bull moose feeding, his long snout buried underwater as he browsed on the grasses growing on the muddy bottom. He caught the movement of the canoe almost instantly, reared his ungainly head with its flat spread of antlers and splashed to shore. In a crash of undergrowth he disappeared among the alders.

'I haven't seen one of those for years,' Finn said. 'They always look to me as though a farm horse mated with an elk.'

She said lightly, 'There's a three-month hunting season on moose, caribou and black bears. It would be wonderful if this whole area were a wildlife sanctuary.'

'You'd lose business—you guide for hunters, don't you?'

'Almost never. I'm working more and more with photographers and film crews—conservationists, people interested in ecotours, that kind of thing... In fact, my next assignment in three weeks is with a film crew from the States. I love watching animals interact with their environment—much more fun than shooting them.'

'Less and less do I understand how you abide Mac,' Finn said tightly. 'He's a hunter to the core.'

Jenessa swiveled on her seat, suddenly tired of this particular misunderstanding. 'Mac and I never have been nor ever will be lovers. The other night we were just—talking.'

As she remembered what they had been talking about, her eyes flashed green, greener by far than the trees behind her head. 'Is that true?' Finn said slowly.

He didn't believe her. 'I suppose if you don't respect women you don't trust them either,' she said caustically.

'The count told me you and Mac had a relationship a couple of years ago. He was very discreet—but it was quite clear what he meant.'

'Well, the count was wrong,' she retorted. 'Finn, we've got to get moving. The last place you want to be in a storm is the middle of a lake.'

His answer was to dig his paddle into the water so that the canoe surged ahead. Thoroughly out of sorts, Jenessa set a killing pace down the lake. She'd told Finn the truth and he hadn't believed her. He'd taken the count's word over hers.

Her father had raised her with a stringent regard for honesty; the flip side of that had been that he had trusted her totally.

Unlike Finn Marston, who didn't trust her at all.

CHAPTER SEVEN

JENESSA and Finn were still an hour away from the campsite when the first gust of wind came whipping over the water, wrinkling the surface like the skin of an old man. A second gust chased the first; the limbs of the spruce trees stirred uneasily. 'We'll keep close to the lee shore,' Jenessa said, feeling a third burst of wind cuff her cheek and flatten her shirt-sleeve to her arm.

Waves gathered, innocent enough at first, then topped with white and spewed with foam. Water slapped the prow and splashed the gear, rocking the canoe on its axis. Then the first fat drops of rain bounced off the lake.

Within minutes the rain was driving into Jenessa's face, almost blinding her. She put all her strength into the blade of her paddle, aware with one corner of her mind of the greater strength of Finn's strokes, aware too of all the demands the day had already placed on both of them.

The last fifteen minutes were pure nightmare, her muscles screaming with tiredness, her body chilled despite the exercise. But finally, calling instructions to Finn over her shoulder, she eased the bow of the canoe into the cove where they were going to camp. Angry waves washed the little beach, whose sand was pitted from the heavy rainfall. The leaves of the birches and alders rattled in the wind. Hopping out of the canoe, Jenessa pulled the bow up on the beach, and steadied it while Finn climbed out. As he came level with her, she saw that his clothes were plastered to his body. His hair clung to his scalp, rain running down his face as if he'd been swimming rather than paddling.

Unexpected laughter gathered in her chest. 'Finn, do I look as awful as you?'

His teeth gleamed white. 'Do you know what I've just realized? I'm paying a hundred dollars a day for the privilege of being soaking wet, dog-tired and starving hungry. I must be out of my mind.'

She was laughing in earnest now, peals of helpless laughter. 'I just put my rates up—today was worth at least two hundred.'

'The way my shoulder muscles feel, you should be paying me.'

A wave washed over her boot, the undertow tugging the sand away beneath her heel. She glanced down and saw to her horror that the canoe was floating broadside to the waves, in danger of swamping. She lunged for the prow, hauled the canoe back up on the beach, and gasped, 'I can't believe I just did that—you never let go of a canoe until it's properly beached. You should fire me for that piece of carelessness.'

'Well,' said Finn. 'Very interesting—so you are capable of neglecting your job.'

For reasons beyond her, he looked extremely pleased with himself. Raindrops stinging her cheeks, she said tartly, 'You wouldn't be looking so happy if all our gear had ended up in the lake. It's going to be dark in half an hour—we'd better hurry.'

They unloaded the canoe and up-ended it in the bushes well away from the water. Then Jenessa led the way through a dense, shadowed thicket of alders, whose branches caught on her pack and whose roots made her stumble for a foothold. From behind her Finn grunted,

'I presume there's a purpose to this? Other than masochism, that is.'

'Trust me,' she said, and with an illogical pang knew how strongly she wanted him to do just that.

Finn said nothing.

Five minutes later the alders ended. Spread in front of them was a grassy meadow sprinkled with wild flowers and tall, white-trunked birches. Jenessa trudged through the knee-high grass, already feeling the wind lessen its bite. Ahead of her loomed a huge outcrop of slate, topped by trees and shrubs. Seeking out a well-remembered crop of birches, she eased her pack to the ground. 'We'll be as sheltered here as anywhere,' she said.

'You sure do know this area,' Finn said appreciatively. 'It's a beautiful place, Jenessa.'

She had last visited it when she was twelve. 'Let's get the tarp up... then we'd better gather some wood before it gets too dark to see what we're doing.'

With her axe she chopped down a dead spruce tree, while Finn dragged fallen birch branches under the tarp. As she was sawing the trunk of the spruce into manageable chunks, he gave a sudden exclamation of pain. 'Ouch—I stubbed my toe! Hey, Jenessa, there's a fireplace already set up here, a whole ring of rocks.'

She let the saw fall, walked over to him and in silence stared down at the circle of stones. Her father had built them. He had been an austere man, little given to fun. But the last time they had camped here he had produced a bag of marshmallows, an unbelievable treat. They had toasted them in the coals until the outsides were a golden-brown and the insides had melted into a smooth, white cream, deliciously sweet. Six months later he was dead...

Dimly she became aware that Finn was gripping her by the shoulders. 'What's wrong? For heaven's sake, tell me what's wrong.'

She stared at him, her eyes haunted by that old grief. Finn didn't look at all like the man who had been responsible for her father's death. But he was that man's grandson, bone of his bone, flesh of his flesh. With a deep shudder she pulled free. 'Nothing,' she muttered.

'You've been here before; I know you have. With Mac?'

That he could be so wrong was more than she could bear. 'Don't, Finn,' she begged. 'Just leave it, please.'

'Yeah—because honesty is something we're avoiding like the plague, you and I,' he said in a voice raw with frustration. 'Let's get the fire going. Then you're going to sit beside it while I put up the tent and find you some dry clothes. I'll cook supper—you'll watch. Do you hear me?'

'I——'

'And don't argue!'

Laughter welled up in her chest again, the kind of laughter that hovered on the very brink of pain. Subduing it, she said meekly, 'All right.'

He looked fiercely protective. Jenessa, who prided herself on her independence, was not used to being protected. She had protected her father more than he her, and Ryan had always had a tendency to push her out into the world rather than shelter her from it. As the flames spewed upward, Finn dragged a log over for her to sit on. His hands pressed on her shoulders with the same paradoxical blend of gentleness and force. 'You're going to sit down and let me look after you,' he said with a crooked smile. 'No matter how difficult it is.'

The rain beat on the tarp, the birches rustled in the wind and the leaping flames made the surrounding darkness all the more impenetrable. She said, with no idea where the words came from, 'I don't understand you at all.'

'You think I understand *you*? Sit, Jenessa—I'll find you some dry clothes.'

She sank down on the log, spreading her hands to the fire's heat, gazing into its vivid, ephemeral brilliance as though it could tell her what she needed to know. After Finn had pitched the tent, she changed into dry clothing, topping them with a soft fleece jacket. He had a line rigged for her wet garments, and was already heating water for tea. By the time she'd hung up her clothes he was ladling chili into a pan, his movements neat and efficient. She hunkered down beside him and rested her fingers on his wrist. 'Finn, I think you should get changed—you can get hypothermia by staying in wet clothes.'

Her fingers were still cold. He clasped them in his, letting his own warmth warm her, and said in a low voice, 'That's the first time you've ever touched me. Apart from shaking hands with me at the motel.'

Into her mind flashed the image of his bare back, its contours both like and yet utterly unlike her own. Would it have been as warm as the fingers curled around hers? Flooded by the same profound unease that she had felt in the tent, Jenessa tugged her hand free. 'I was worried about you, that's all,' she said, and watched him take her words at face value.

'I just wish——' he said violently. 'Hell, what's the use? I'll be back in a minute.'

When he came back she handed him a mug of hot tea. The chili was bubbling gently on the metal grill and she had wrapped the last of the rolls in foil to heat. 'After today we have some very strong curried beef,' she remarked, 'then it's dried food and whatever fish we can catch.'

'So I'd better enjoy the chili, is that what you're saying?'

'You got it.' She sipped her tea, feeling warm and dry and comfortable. 'This beats portaging; that's the trouble with cedar canoes—they're heavy. But I love their lines.'

They chatted about canoes and orienteering as they ate, as though by an unspoken agreement a truce had been called on any incendiary subjects. Or, Jenessa wondered, was their new camaraderie simply the result of having survived together the trials of the day?

The answer didn't seem very important. Letting herself enjoy Finn's undoubted intelligence, laughing at his wit and arguing amicably with some of his opinions, she relaxed into the sheer pleasure of his company. After stoking up the fire, they did the dishes, by which time Jenessa was openly yawning. 'Don't take it personally,' she gaped. 'You're far from boring. But it seems a very long time since I got up this morning.'

'Sleep well,' he said casually. 'I'm going to stay here for a while.'

'I—thank you, Finn,' she said clumsily.

The firelight threw moving shadows over his face; his smile was singularly sweet, touching something deep within her. 'No problem. Off you go.'

He had stashed their packs, which were very wet, in the vestibule of the tent. But the sleeping-bags were still placed a careful distance apart. Jenessa undressed, curled up in the soft folds of down and fell asleep.

* * *

She awoke to the wind flapping the walls of the tent. It was still dark, a darkness pierced up by the glow of the campfire. The illuminated dial of her waterproof watch told her it was almost an hour past midnight. Rolling over, she saw that the other sleeping-bag was empty: Finn was still up.

She had gone to bed three hours ago. What was he doing?

Sliding out of her bag, she crept to the entrance of the tent, where the wind brushed her skin with its cool fingers. Finn was still sitting on the log, in profile to her. He was hunched over, his head buried in his hands, his elbows resting on his knees.

The long curve of his spine expressed both despair and defeat—feelings that struck Jenessa to the heart, for in her life she had known both intimately. Finn, she knew, would not thank her for observing such private emotions.

Yet she was conscious of a strong urge to walk over to him, to rub the tension from his shoulders and help him bear whatever was attacking him.

The last thing he looked was ruthless.

As quietly as she could she backed into the tent again. Her sleeping-bag was still warm; she huddled into it, feeling helpless and unhappy. Perhaps it was grief she had seen, grief for the man called Jim.

That very day a circle of stones had called up her own grief for her father. But she hadn't shared it with Finn; so what right did she have to intrude on his?

None whatsoever.

Flat on her back, her eyes wide open, she watched as the flames sank lower and lower. There was a sudden hiss of steam as Finn dumped water on the coals. Turning her back, she burrowed her face in her sweater just as he crawled into the tent. She tried to breathe naturally, as though she were asleep, and heard the small intimate sounds of a man undressing in the darkness.

The zipper on his sleeping-bag rasped. Then there was only the voice of the wind in the night.

Eventually Jenessa fell asleep. From long habit she woke at dawn, and was instantly awake. The tent walls bulged and flattened and bulged again as the wind gusted through the trees; the birch leaves gossiped, busy-tongued, and the tarp rattled self-importantly. She and Finn wouldn't be going anywhere today, she thought, already dreading a whole day spent around the campsite in his company. What would they talk about? What tasks could she invent to fill the long hours from dawn to dusk?

Restlessly she turned over, then recoiled with instinctive haste. In the night Finn had rolled off his insulated sleeping-pad; he was sprawled only inches away from her. His head rested on his arm, while his bare chest rose and fell with the slow rhythm of his breathing. His eyes were closed.

Jenessa lay still, her own breath caught in her throat. Often enough she had heard the euphemistic phrase 'sleeping together'; until now she had never applied it to herself. Yet here she was, literally face to face with a man who had spent the night at her side.

Ruth and Stevie slept together, in the big bed covered with the green and white quilt that Ruth's grandmother had stitched in a pattern traditional to the Newfoundland outports. But Ruth and Stevie also made love in that bed. An entirely separate activity, or so Jenessa had always thought.

Now, as she studied Finn's face feature by feature, her tidy little categories began to fall away. His face, asleep, was of course still his face. Yet there were very real, if subtle differences between what she saw now and what she was accustomed to seeing. He looked younger, for one thing. Younger and—she sought for the right word—defenceless, that was it. Awake, he hid behind barriers that allowed her so far and no further. Asleep, she realized with a peculiar ache of her heart, he drew her to him rather than pushed her away.

The relaxed curve of his mouth fascinated her. His fingers, loosely curled, were almost touching the sweater she was using as a pillow; she could see the steady throb of the pulse in his wrist and the blue veins that meandered up his arm. His body hair was almost black, springing from his forearm, furring his deep chest. There was a white, indented scar below the hollow of his collarbone.

Within her a small trembling began, like the quivering of aspen leaves in the lightest of winds. Her movements as uncertain and as wary as those of a caribou calf newborn among the aspens, Jenessa stretched out her hand and rested a single fingertip on Finn's wrist.

The blood pulsed slowly and powerfully against her skin, the very voice of his heart. Her own pulse leaped to meet it and a flush crept into her cheeks. She let her fingers wrap around his wrist, encompassing it, feeling through every nerve in her body the hardness of bone and the heat of his skin. Small enough sensations, yet they felt astoundingly, unbelievably intimate.

He stirred very slightly, making a tiny sound in his sleep. She snatched her hand back, scarcely breathing, waiting for his eyes to snap open and all the barriers to reassert themselves, driving her away. Then, almost imperceptibly, he sank back into the depths of sleep.

Her quickened heartbeat was like that of a frightened bird. She could have rolled over and sought sleep again; she could have got up, taken her clothes and left the tent. Instead she felt her hand, of its own volition, drift across the small space that separated her from Finn and curve itself around his ribcage.

Again there was the tautness of bone and the warmth of flesh under her palm. A man's flesh, Jenessa thought in confusion. But not just any man's: Finn's.

A bittersweet ache blossomed to life between her thighs. Blossomed and spread and grew in its demands, its ancient impulsions. As the blood throbbed through her veins, Jenessa's eyes widened in true surprise. I want him, she thought, and heard the three small words echo and re-echo in her brain even as they were surging through her body. I want to make love with Finn... I want to lie with him and learn what his body feels like close to mine. I want to be initiated—guided by him—into that mysterious land where a man and woman come together in the act of love.

I belong, she thought dazedly. I'm not a misfit any more. I understand now why Ruth's face is lit up the morning after Stevie comes home from a long trip. Because I want the same thing to happen to me.

Her lips curved in a joyful smile. All those years of feeling like an outcast had vanished, dissipated by the closeness of one man's body. She felt like singing. She felt like dancing under the birch trees where the wind whistled through the grass. She also felt, she admitted with an honesty that made her blush, like closing the distance between her and Finn so that they lay breast to chest and hip to hip. What would that feel like?

Finn muttered something under his breath, shifting restlessly. Jenessa drew her hand back, terrified that he would waken and ask her what she was doing, holding her breath as he stretched, the muscles pulled taut over his belly. Then, the sleeping-bag rucked around his waist, he rolled over, sighed and lay still again.

With a spasm of agony that was as sharp as it was absurd, Jenessa felt as though she had been exiled, driven from a place she had scarcely begun to explore. Left alone again—as all her life she had been alone, she realized with painful truth. Although her father had raised her with punctilious care, he had rarely expressed his affection overtly, and Ryan, a bachelor by choice, had been perfectly happy adding rooms to his house and carving duck decoys before she had arrived on his doorstep at the age of sixteen.

She didn't like the tenor of her thoughts. The confines of the tent suddenly seemed claustrophobic, and Finn's closeness was a threat rather than a source of pleasure. Waiting until she was sure he was sound asleep again, she rummaged for her toilet articles in her pack, picked up her clean clothes and sneaked out of the tent.

Despite the wind the air was warmer than it had been last night and she badly needed a bath. In daylight she found an easier path through the alders to the beach. The waves were high, too high for safe canoeing, and it was an act of courage to strip off her clothes and plunge into the cool waters of the lake with her soap and shampoo; she ducked to rinse herself off and waded to shore. As she scrubbed herself dry, she found herself looking down at her body with new eyes.

A woman's body. But what would Finn think of it? Her only standards of comparison came from the magazines that so intimidated her. She didn't have the big breasts of a movie star. She wasn't skinny like the sleek, aloof models who were garbed in outfits that would have been useless in the woods. Her toenails weren't painted. She wore no jewelry.

She did have a recognizable hairstyle, she thought ruefully, starting to pull on her clothes. But what did it matter? If she had awakened to her sexuality in the tent beside Finn, she had also been shot through with terror at the prospect of him discovering how she felt. Nothing was going to happen. Nothing.

The last thing she wanted him to see was the change in her.

She trekked back to the campsite, made another trip to the lake for water and started a fire. She was splitting kindling with her hatchet when Finn emerged from the tent, pulling on his shirt. With a huge effort Jenessa dragged her eyes away from the flat planes of his belly, and said in a voice that sounded horribly sprightly, 'Good morning.'

Although he shot her a disconcertingly sharp glance, all he said was, 'When are we leaving?'

'We aren't. The winds are forty kilometers an hour and the next lake is far more exposed than this one.'

'So what are we going to do?'

'Nothing.'

'Jenessa, we can't sit here for a whole day!'

Voicing some of her own frustration, she said, 'Finn, we can't arrange nature to suit ourselves.'

'What in heaven's name will we do all day?'

She wished she had the answer. 'Sit and smell the golden rod,' she said flippantly.

'Oh, for God's sake! I can't take forever for this trip—there's a real world out there and it has more important things on its mind than the way the wind's blowing.'

'This is the real world,' Jenessa said, her green eyes openly unfriendly.

Finn was doing up the buttons on his shirt, the movement of his fingers jerky with impatience. 'Don't be ridiculous—the wilderness is escapism, pure and simple.'

Only an hour ago Jenessa had fantasized lying in Finn's arms. She must have been out of her mind. 'This is as real as the world gets,' she snapped. 'If you can't handle it, that's your problem.'

He stepped closer, his irises almost black with anger. 'Just what do you mean by that?'

'You're scared to death you might come face to face with yourself out here! Because there's nowhere to run, is there, Finn? No distractions, no multi-million-dollar company taking every minute of every day of your life. No telephones, no meetings, no oil-wells. There's only wind and water and trees and your own thoughts to keep you company—and you can't stand that. That's what I mean.'

'You couldn't be more wrong!'

She said very quietly, 'Who's Jim?'

The colour drained from Finn's face. In a strangled voice he said, 'Who told you about Jim?'

Already regretting her question, Jenessa stood her ground. 'You did. Yesterday morning you were dreaming, and said his name.'

'And ever since you've just been waiting for the chance to bring it up,' he accused, hunching his shoulders and jamming his hands in the pockets of his jeans.

Hurt, she cried, 'I wasn't! But you can't run away out here, Finn—that's what the wilderness does; it takes away all the distractions and lets you listen to the silence.'

'How poetic,' he sneered. 'Don't tell me you're not into escapism, Jenessa Reed. You're nearly twenty-six years old and oblivious to your own sexuality—I call that running away.'

It hardly seemed the time to tell him that only an hour ago she had stopped running. 'I wish you'd tell me who Jim is,' she persisted. 'Maybe it would help if you talked about him.'

'Why don't you just mind your own business?'

And what reply could she make to that? Employees weren't supposed to tell their employers to go to hell. Glaring at him, she said, 'I'm going to cook the last of the bacon and eggs. Coffee or tea?'

'Coffee. Are you really serious that we can't go anywhere today?'

'Go take a look at the lake,' she said, exasperated. 'Guides are discouraged from drowning their clients. More's the pity.'

A reluctant smile tugged at Finn's lips. 'Your eyes are the same colour as the birch leaves when you're angry,' he said.

The sculpted line of his mouth fascinated her, and she had always found his smile irresistible. 'Yours are like stones,' she blurted with more accuracy than tact, and bent to put a log on the fire.

The flames licked hungrily at the wood and Finn, as she had requested, marched toward the alders to look at the lake.

It was only seven-thirty. Twenty-four hours to go, she thought, and wondered how in the world she was going to get through the day.

CHAPTER EIGHT

BREAKFAST was eaten largely in silence. Afterwards Finn set out to gather more wood, and as she washed the dishes Jenessa heard the steady thunk of the axe reverberating among the trees. Finn wasn't about to smell the golden rod, she thought bitterly. His restlessness seemed to have infected her: she reorganized the food bags, rinsed out some clothes and swept the floor of the tent, placing the sleeping-bags as far apart as she could. By now Finn had stacked a neat pile of logs by the fireplace. 'I'm going for a walk along the shore,' he said.

She watched him stride away between the trees. He hadn't suggested that she go with him. Hating herself for minding, she settled herself on a log by the fire and opened the one book she had brought. Ruth had loaned it to her, recommending it as a good read. But the characters seemed to spend an awful lot of time taking off high-couture clothes and, in various adulterous combinations, climbing between satin sheets; the graphic descriptions of what went on between those sheets made Jenessa even more restless.

She had never done any of those things. But her imagination seemed to have sprung to life along with her body, and all too well she could picture doing them with Finn.

Maybe Ruth had recommended the book on purpose, she thought crossly. Next time she'd bring a textbook on forest management.

She made tuna sandwiches with pita bread for lunch, ate alone, and was just starting to worry about Finn when he appeared through the alders. 'You've been a long time,' she commented noncommittally.

He sat down and took the sandwich she held out to him. 'You'll laugh if I tell you what I've been doing.'

His lean fingers clasping the sandwich made her shiver with inner awareness. No satin sheets here, and no couture clothes either, she thought with a touch of desperate humour. She was in a bad way when a man eating a tuna fish sandwich made her feel like jumping on him. 'I won't laugh.'

'There's a cove half a mile from here that's in the lee of the wind. I sat on a rock and watched the water. There were tadpoles there, big ones—potential bullfrogs, I suppose. One of them had a tail like ribbon and two back legs with perfectly formed feet. No front legs yet, but you could see them just beneath the skin, and I found myself wondering how they came out.' He took a bite of the sandwich and gave a dry laugh. 'Never thought I'd find myself curious about bullfrogs.'

He looked relaxed in a way new to her. The muscles in his throat moved as he swallowed; she watched them, wondering what it would be like to slide her lips down the corded tendons. In comparison to some of the sexual gymnastics described in Ruth's book, it was a relatively mild ambition, yet it filled her with a wild, sweet longing.

'What's the matter?' Finn said sharply.

'Nothing! I—I was getting worried about you, that's all.'

'You look kind of jumpy—perhaps *you* should go and watch the tadpoles.'

She scrambled to her feet. 'I think I will go for a walk,' she said. 'See you later.'

He fingered his chin. 'I'll shave while you're gone.'

Jenessa took off as though a black bear were on her trail. She tramped along the rocky shore, feeling the wind cool her cheeks. She had to settle down. She couldn't spend the next two weeks wanting to tear the clothes off Finn's body every time he came within ten feet of her. It was ridiculous. She'd never behaved like this before. Never.

Maybe there were advantages to being a misfit.

She walked hard for well over an hour. Then she turned back, taking her time, in no hurry to face Finn again. If he had discerned—and been unflattered by—her total lack of any sexual response to him up until now, would he not also recognize the change in her? And if he did, how would he act?

Flights of imagination were one thing. In actuality she was in no hurry to find out.

She came round the last bend, where the trail led through the alders. Three caribou—a stag and two cows—were swimming away from her toward the middle of the lake.

Finn should see this. She ducked into the alders, running, her feet dodging roots, her hands grabbing for holds among the branches. She was at the very end of the trail, jumping to avoid a mud puddle, when she saw a pair of large rubber boots right in front of her. With a gasp of dismay, her momentum carrying her forward, she thudded into the man who had just entered the trail. He dropped the metal pot he was carrying and wrapped his arms around her to keep her from falling.

He was bare-chested. As imagination and reality fused, Jenessa was flooded with a host of sensations, some of which she couldn't have begun to imagine, so far were they from her experience. The hardness of his chest, bruising the bridge of her nose. The rasp of his body hair under her cheek. The strength of his arms around her ribcage and the dig of his fingers in her spine.

She closed her eyes, the better to savor his warmth and solidity, her body as fluid a curve as the grass in the wind. His skin smelled clean and indefinably masculine; without even thinking how he might interpret her actions, she rubbed her cheek against his chest and flattened her palms on his back.

'Jenessa,' Finn whispered hoarsely. 'Jenessa...' He raised her chin with one hand, his eyes widening at the rapt delight in her face. Then, almost instantly, they darkened with purpose. 'You don't know how often I've wanted to do this,' he muttered, and lowered his mouth to hers.

Jenessa might be inexperienced, but she was by no means imperceptive. Beneath the beginnings of Finn's kiss there was real hunger; his brief restraint gave her the time to feel to the fullest an answering surge of passion whose intensity was unlike anything she had ever felt before. She had no training in coyness or subterfuge; she allowed her hunger full rein, and felt the shock run through his frame.

Then his lips were roving hers, teasing them open with the fierce impatience so characteristic of him, and she felt the first touch of his tongue. With a small sound of pleasure she let her hands slide up his spine, her fingers burying themselves in the silky hair at his nape. He strained her closer, until the softness of her breasts was crushed to his chest, and his kiss deepened.

Dizzily she wondered how she had lived this long without ever suspecting that such pleasure lay in store for her. Her tongue danced with his even as his hands roamed her body, tracing the sweep of her spine and the slender lines of her waist. Then he drew her hips against his, and with true wonder she felt the hardness of his erection.

Pulling back a little, she whispered, 'I did that to you?'

Finn gave an exultant laugh, drinking in the flush high on her cheekbones, the brilliance of her eyes and the softness of the lips that he had laid claim to. 'Indeed you did—do you wonder?'

Her peal of laughter climbed with his. She said artlessly, 'Of course I do. I've never felt like this before, Finn—never! It's wonderful; I love it.'

'You mean that, don't you?' he said slowly. 'Whatever's happened, Jenessa? You've acted like a stick of wood around me up until now—what changed you so suddenly?'

It never occurred to her to lie. Her flush spreading, she said, 'This morning when I woke up you were lying so close to me that—I don't know how to explain it. I guess you looked like a man who could sit and watch tadpoles rather than someone who was the owner of a big business. I—I just knew I wanted you, that's all,' she finished lamely.

'Did you touch me?' he flashed.

'Well... yes.'

'So I wasn't dreaming...' With a primitive edge of triumph in his voice that brushed her with unease, he said, 'Come here.'

'Finn, I——'

His kiss prevented her from saying anything else—a kiss that made her head whirl and her body clamor for more. Before she could totally lose control, she gasped, 'We can't——'

'I want to make love to you. Here and now.' He nuzzled at her throat. 'Well, not right here—in the tent.'

He looked so sure of himself, so certain that she would capitulate. 'I only met you a week ago; we can't——'

'That's got nothing to do with it,' he said forcefully. 'If you were a little more experienced, you'd know that this kind of sexual chemistry doesn't happen often and that we'd be fools not to take advantage of it.'

'But I am inexperienced and——'

'I'll fix that,' Finn said.

Jenessa was beginning to get angry and couldn't have said exactly why. Fumbling for clarity, she said, 'I'm not a commodity on the stock market that you buy when the price is right... I'm a person. With feelings. I'm not even sure you like me, Finn—only two days ago you were accusing me of making love with Mac.'

'I've changed my mind. I don't think you did.'

'Just like that?' she said indignantly. 'You might have told me. Anyway, we can't make love—I might get pregnant.'

'I'll fix that, too.'

'How?' she said blankly.

'The usual way, Jenessa—I went to the drugstore before we left.'

'You mean you *planned* this?'

He said irritably, 'Stop putting the worst interpretation on everything I say. The first time I saw you, there was something about you that attracted me. I was pretty sure two weeks in the woods with you would increase, not decrease that attraction. So I came prepared.' He shrugged. 'I'm no more anxious to produce offspring than you are.'

His language reduced what she was feeling to the lowest common denominator. Jenessa pulled away from him, grabbing at a branch for balance. 'You might have been attracted to me, but you didn't like me.' With sudden intuition she added, 'I don't think you like women at all...like them any more than you respect them.'

'I'm sorry I ever said that!'

The words out before she had time to think, she asked, 'Were you ever married?' Her stomach clenched. 'Or are you married now?'

He raked his fingers through his hair. 'No. Of course not.'

'How old are you?'

'Thirty-five.'

'Then there's no of course about it,' she retorted, ripping a piece of bark from the branch. Desire had died in her, leaving her tense and on edge, and very much back in the world of reality. Yes, Finn's mother had committed suicide when Finn was still a teenager; but that would have been cause for pity, surely, not disrespect. And she, Jenessa, wasn't supposed to know about it, any more than she was supposed to know that he owned the very ground they were standing on.

The metal pot was wedged among the alder trunks at her feet. 'Were you going for water?' she asked at random.

'Yeah...until you ran into me. It's time you stopped running; you know that as well as I do.'

'There were three caribou swimming across the lake. I wanted you to see them.'

Finn said levelly, 'Come to bed with me, Jenessa. Now.'

His voice was dispassionate. But his eyes burned into hers, dark with purpose, and unconsciously she swayed toward him, the very beat of her blood echoing that purpose. But this time a small part of her brain stayed detached from desire; it saw triumph flare in his face, and shouted her a warning. 'How could you have been attracted to me when you didn't even like me?' she demanded.

'You're upset because I went to the drugstore, aren't you? Nothing very romantic about that, I agree. But I'd argue it shows more respect for you than if I fell on you in the wilderness without a thought for the consequences.'

It was a strange moment to remember how Stevie—sturdy, inarticulate Stevie—had braved a lingerie store in a St John's mall because Ruth wanted a lacy black nightgown for Christmas. Jenessa said, 'We don't love each other.'

'That's another romantic fallacy,' Finn said impatiently. 'Fifty percent of the couples who swear undying love at the altar end up in the divorce courts. Spare me that one.'

He was implying that she was both naïve and ignorant; and he could be right on both counts. 'You sound so cold-blooded,' she cried. 'This book Ruth loaned me... the characters get in and out of bed with as little thought as if they were changing their socks. There has to be more to it than that!'

'I don't behave that way—never have. It's been a long time since I've been with a woman.'

'Oh,' Jenessa said, her face brightening, 'I see. Then you're like a stag caribou in the rutting season—it's been a year since he mounted a cow, so there's nothing particularly subtle about the way he behaves.'

'I'm not a goddamned caribou—I'm a man!' Finn exploded. 'You have to be the most argumentative woman I've ever come across.'

'You mean I'm not falling flat on my back after one kiss.'

He kicked at the nearest alder, his boot churning up murky waves in the puddle. 'I wouldn't recommend you do that here,' he said sarcastically. 'But I'm getting the message—the answer's no. I'm going to get water, Jenessa—but we're not finished with this.'

She didn't suppose they were. Which didn't make her feel any happier.

As Finn disappeared down the trail, she wandered back to the campsite. His towel and shaving kit were sitting on the log; he had been, she realized belatedly, clean-shaven. The better to kiss you, my dear, she thought, and wished she had never sighted the three caribou.

Leaving him a note on the log, she took a container and went to pick blueberries. She liked picking berries; it was a very soothing activity. When she came back, Finn was chopping kindling. He was, she was glad to see, now wearing a shirt. She said casually, 'Salmon pasta with blueberry cobbler for dessert; how does that sound?'

He straightened to his full height, the hatchet balanced in his right hand. 'Jenessa, I'm not going to let you act as though you never kissed me. It happened and we're not going to pretend it didn't.'

Ruthless, she thought with a shiver along her spine. As ruthless as the grandson of George Hilchey would have to be. With a rebellious lift of her chin she said, 'You're right—it happened. Past tense. Which is where it belongs.'

He stepped closer. She clutched the container of blueberries to her chest, saw him bend his head and felt his lips brush hers. The shiver ran along her nerves this time, as ruthless in its own demands as he was in his. She flared, 'I'm not going to sleep with you or go to bed with you or make love with you—whatever words you want to use. I'm not going to!'

'We'll see about that,' Finn said. 'We'll be together at least another ten days. And nights.'

Jenessa looked at him in silence. He was stronger than she; she knew that already. Stronger, heavier and infinitely more experienced. But she was damned if she was going to show George Hilchey's grandson that she was afraid of him. Putting the pot of blueberries carefully on the grass, she said, 'Would you rather have dried peas or fresh carrots with the pasta?'

'Carrots. It's your own life you're limiting, Jenessa.'

That she had already thought of that didn't help at all. 'You sure don't like having a woman turn you down.'

With a flick of his wrist he flung the hatchet at the log. The blade bit into the wood, the handle quivering. 'No, I don't,' he said savagely. 'Not when the woman's you.'

Her heart gave an uncomfortable leap in her chest. 'Don't give me that line. You don't like or respect me, remember?'

'I don't know how the devil I feel about you,' Finn snarled. He picked up the big axe and began splitting the birch logs lying in the grass, every move imbued with violence.

Whatever he felt, it wasn't indifference, Jenessa thought, and clamped her tongue down before she could mouth the words. She built up the fire and began assembling the ingredients for the dessert, and the whole time while she was cooking and eating and cleaning up afterwards she was aware of him watching her. She lit the propane lamp and read more of her book, and at ten o'clock said with an artificial yawn, 'I think I'll hit the sack.'

'Me too,' said Finn.

Panic flared in her breast. 'Don't look like that,' he rasped. 'I'm not into rape. But I'm not into you denying what happened between us earlier today, either.'

She turned the lamp off, doused the fire and by the light of her flashlight crawled into the tent, Finn on her heels. The tent had never seemed so small nor Finn so large. Nor, she thought honestly, pulling off her socks, her own feelings so ambivalent. Dragging her sweater over her head, she folded it for a pillow, then twisted to place it at the head of her sleeping-bag, the flashlight illuminating the tautness of her T-shirt across her breasts.

A quality in the silence alerted her to what Finn was seeing. Blushing scarlet, she said in a strangled voice, 'Goodnight,' and turned off the flashlight. But as she struggled with her bush pants in the darkness, then slid into her sleeping-bag, the emotion that played itself through her body was not fear, embarrassment or anger, or even sexual frustration—nothing that she would have expected. It was compassion. For the look she had caught, fleetingly, on Finn's face had been that of a man in exile. A man who for a long time had been banished from what his heart, at its deepest level, craved.

She didn't understand the source or the intensity of that look. She did know it was real.

During the night the wind changed direction, bringing sunny skies and a tailwind the next morning as Jenessa and Finn paddled up the lake. The two portages were short and they were early reaching the place she wanted to camp, a small plateau on the barrens edged with granite outcrops and low hills. 'Tomorrow we start out the day with a portage—short but steep,' she said as they hauled the canoe up on the shore. 'There's a waterfall only a half a mile from here called Osprey Falls; you can shower in it if you want.'

While Finn went off to look for wood, Jenessa pitched the tent in a circle of junipers whose feathery branches swayed gently in the breeze. She planned the evening meal and built a fire pit and rolled over a couple of rocks for her and Finn to sit on, and still he hadn't come back. She couldn't hear the whine of the saw or the thwack of the axe. Frowning a little to herself, she made her way through the junipers and spruce trees to the edge of the barrens, treading soft-footed by instinct.

She saw Finn first. He was crouched on the fringe of the trees, gazing out over the barrens, his hands loose on his knees, his face intent. The axe was lying at his feet. With exquisite care she inched forward and saw what he was watching—a small herd of caribou not fifty yards away, upwind from them, grazing on the lichens. The stag was in his prime, his antlers sweeping forward over his dark-furred muzzle and back over his pale, powerful shoulders; the cows were sleek and healthy, their hooves clicking as they ranged over the hummocks.

Very slowly she sank down beside Finn, sensing him take in her presence. The herd came closer, until she could hear the animals chewing and see the separate hairs on the bull's ruff and the liquid darkness of his eye; the sunlight gleamed on his flanks.

An hour passed. The sun sank in the sky, bathing the barrens in a soft gold light. A flock of chickadees foraged in the spruce trees next to Finn, chattering back and forth to each other. High in the sky an eagle traced big, lazy circles, then sloped off into the hills.

The caribou had been moving steadily to the south, and finally the last of them ambled out of sight. Easing out the stiffness in his knees, Finn got to his feet. He smiled at Jenessa, his face peaceful and unguarded. 'Beautiful creatures—I've never seen them so close before.'

'They're in good shape this year.'

Lazily he stretched his shoulders. 'I left a pile of wood back there in the bushes... I'd better find some more.'

'No hurry,' she said tranquilly. 'I love the barrens; you can almost hear the silence, can't you?'

Finn hesitated. Then he said, 'I'm sorry about last night, Jenessa. You stunned me when you kissed me in the alders... knocked me sideways. So I pushed you too hard and got angry when you didn't cooperate. I knew it at the time but I couldn't seem to stop.'

The last thing she had expected from him was such a straightforward apology. 'You're forgiven,' she said, and knew her lightly spoken words for the truth.

He hesitated again. 'You're a virgin.'

Her lashes flickered. 'Anachronistic of me, isn't it?'

His gaze lingered over her slim figure, gilded by the setting sun. 'Nothing's changed—I still want you. But I might as well tell you that marriage has never been in my books, any more than falling in love has been. They're not for me.'

Jenessa had never thought they were for her, either. But until Finn had kissed her yesterday she had sometimes wondered if she was asexual, so totally out of touch had she been with that side of her nature. Yesterday she had discovered that she was not out of touch at all. So perhaps love and marriage were no longer out of reach, any more than sex was.

But not love and marriage with Finn. He had just made that very clear.

Her brow furrowed in thought. She had often watched caribou mate in the autumn out on the barrens: brief, powerful and instinctual couplings, male joining to female with a natural and wild beauty. Maybe that was what Finn was to her. A mate. A mate who would then go his own way, and she hers, as was the way of the wilderness.

Sunlight and shadow barred his face. Which man was he? The man she saw now, a proud man, still reticent in his honesty...or the man she had seen last night, harsh, angry and demanding?

Troubled, she murmured, 'I know so little about you.'

He ran his fingers along the green springs of a juniper, then looked out over the barrens and the gently rising hills. 'I own all this,' he said abruptly. 'All the land we'll see in the two weeks we're together—it's mine.'

Again he had surprised her. With matching honesty she said, 'I know—Mac told me. You inherited it from your grandfather.'

Finn grimaced. 'You want me to keep it as a wildlife sanctuary. Mac wants to buy it as a hunting reserve. Forestry companies want it for the trees, and mining outfits for the minerals. I was dead sure of one thing when I came—I didn't want it.'

Dry-mouthed, she said, 'And do you still feel that way?'

He said wryly, 'I never took the time to watch tadpoles—or caribou—until I came here. Whatever that means.' Moving his shoulders restlessly, he added, 'I'm going to get more wood before it gets dark.'

'I'll carry back what you found and start a fire.'

He led her through the trees to a tangled heap of dead branches, helping her load them in her arms. Then, as she was standing there fully laden, he said, 'Got you, Jenessa,' leaned forward and kissed her, a kiss of leisurely and deliberate sensuality.

This time Jenessa knew what to expect and recklessly met him halfway, their mouths clinging together for long moments during which, for Jenessa at least, time seemed to stop. When he finally moved back, she was trembling from head to foot.

Picking up the axe, flashing her a smile, Finn said, 'See you later.'

Infuriated, she demanded, 'Am I the only one who feels as if I've been charged by a whole herd of caribou? That the sun's come out after six weeks of rain?'

'Darling Jenessa, if that pile of wood weren't in the way, you'd know precisely what you do to me. Don't burn the supper, will you?'

'Darling Jenessa'... Mouth hanging open, Jenessa stared after him as he disappeared through the trees. The wood was heavy. She trudged back to the campsite and started supper.

CHAPTER NINE

THE next morning Jenessa woke at first light. There was not a breath of wind. A hot, sunny day, she thought, burying her face in her sleeping-bag. Mosquitoes. Blackflies. Three portages. Maybe I'll go back to sleep...

'Good morning,' Finn said.

She raised her sleep-flushed face, her hair tousled. He was leaning on one elbow watching her with such open pleasure that her heart skipped a beat. 'Hello,' she muttered, rubbing her eyes.

'What's on the agenda for today?'

'I'm going to have a quick shower at the waterfall. Then we should leave right after breakfast; we've got quite a way to go today.' Today they would come within ten miles of the boundary of what had once been her father's property. But she wasn't going to tell Finn that.

'I'll go with you—to the waterfall, I mean.'

'I'm going to shower,' she repeated. 'You can't!'

His eyes dancing, he said, 'Cold water discourages passion—you'll be quite safe.'

'I don't think this has much to do with safety,' Jenessa said vigorously.

'Shower with a friend and save water.'

'An admirable sentiment that doesn't apply to waterfalls.'

'We're wasting time arguing.' Openly laughing at her, Finn added, 'I might get lost if I try and find the waterfall on my own. And you shouldn't let me swim alone—I bet both those rules are in the guide handbook.'

A desperate shyness was urging her to stay at the campsite and have breakfast ready for Finn when he came back from the waterfall. Grabbing for her bush pants, Jenessa hauled them on inside her sleeping-bag, an action she knew was truly silly when in ten minutes she might be stripping everything off in front of him. She unzippered the bag, gathered her toilet articles and clean clothes and said peevishly, 'Let's go.'

A clearly demarcated animal trail wound through the woods toward Osprey Falls. Jenessa led the way, walking very fast, the roar of the waterfall growing louder and louder. The trail soon emerged beside the pool at the base of the falls. Finn said softly, 'How beautiful...'

At the far side of the pool, from a thirty-foot drop, water swept over the boulders, spewing white foam that was shot through with the delicate hues of a rainbow. On the near side ledges of rock split and gentled the force of the water; graceful ferns overhung a series of cascades as white as snow. Tall fir trees enclosed the falls, puncturing the depthless blue of the sky; the same blue shimmered on the surface of the pool.

It was indeed beautiful, as beautiful as she remembered it. She said brusquely, 'I'm surprised you haven't had any offers from the power company. They could build a dam here. Concrete and steel, right up your alley.'

'Don't, Jenessa—not here.'

'What—a businessmen letting sentiment get in the way of profits?' she mocked.

'Thanks for reminding me,' he retorted. 'Since I happen to own this waterfall, I'm going to have a shower in it. You can do what you like.'

'Pulling rank on me, Finn?' she flashed.

'Yeah, that's exactly what I'm doing. Go back to the camp and make breakfast, why don't you?'

Tossing her head, knowing she was behaving disgracefully, Jenessa said, 'Make me.'

He advanced on her, pulling his T-shirt out of the waistband of his jeans, his mouth a thin line. Before he could touch her, she said in a rush, 'I'm scared to death; that's why I'm being so bitchy.'

Finn stopped in his tracks. Then he ran his hands across the width of her shoulders, where the muscles were bunched with tension. 'In about three minutes the mosquitoes are going to find us, and I can't imagine that making love on a rock-ledge under a waterfall would be an experience you'd enjoy. You're as safe as you could be, Jenessa.' His voice roughened. 'I guess this wasn't such a great idea. I just want to see you naked, that's all.'

Just, she thought crazily. As if it were nothing at all. 'We have to get on that flat ledge that's level with the pool,' she muttered. 'The water only drops about ten feet there.'

With none of her usual agility she crashed through the bushes toward the ledge. When she could go no further without actually stepping on to the wet rock, she turned to face Finn, as panic-stricken as an animal at bay. 'I can't do this,' she wailed. 'I'm not sophisticated like the women in Ruth's book. I've never...'

Her voice died away, because for once Finn looked at a loss. 'You're terrified, aren't you?' he said flatly. 'I didn't mean to frighten you—it's the last thing I wanted to do. I'll have a quick swim in the pool, then I'll go back and start breakfast while you shower...okay?'

Taking her silence for consent, he pulled his T-shirt over his head and kicked off his boots. Then he unbuckled his leather belt and reached for the zipper on his jeans, his hand brushing the white scar on his belly.

I *am* running away, Jenessa thought. Running because this is unknown territory and I can't guess its dangers. But if there are dangers, there might also be rewards. Do I want to run from them too?

Taking a deep breath to give herself courage, she put her haversack on the ground and took off her own boots. Then she undid her bush pants and let them slide down her hips, stepping out of them. Finn seized her by the wrist. 'Jenessa . . . what are you doing?'

He could see what she was doing, and he was not a stupid man. 'I've stopped running,' she said.

'You've got guts,' he said slowly. 'My God, you've got guts.' Molding her shoulders in his hands, he kissed her parted lips, a brief kiss that in its careful lack of demands both acknowledged her fears and did its best to allay them.

Connection, Jenessa thought dimly. Touch. That was what she had needed. She wrapped her arms around Finn's waist and rested her cheek on his chest, feeling the roughness of his body hair, already familiar to her, and the heavy pounding of his heart. 'That feels better,' she said.

He pushed her away a little so that he could see her face and said with a catch of laughter, 'I wonder if I'll ever be able to anticipate what you'll do next?' Then, as naturally as if the two of them had done this many times before, he drew her T-shirt over her head.

She hadn't bothered with a bra. Her breasts, small, high-pointed and firm, shone like silk in the early morning light. Finn said huskily, 'You're more beautiful than I could have imagined.'

Standing a little taller, Jenessa said artlessly, 'Really?'

'Really.' Grinning, he added, 'However, a cold shower is definitely becoming imperative, and there's a mosquito hovering round your left ear. Let's go.'

With an ease she wouldn't have thought possible a few minutes ago, Jenessa slid out of her bikini pants. Finn's jeans and briefs had joined his T-shirt on the ground; for a moment, forgetting the mosquitoes and her own shyness, she gazed at him in silence.

His bruised ribs and deep chest tapered to narrow hips and long legs imbued with a lean strength. Flushing a little, she saw that he did indeed need a cold shower. It was one thing, she thought, to have seen photographs of Greek sculptures, another to have a man of flesh and blood standing naked in front of her. Her green eyes very clear, she said, 'You're beautiful, too.'

Again, Finn looked taken aback. He was not normally a man who lacked for words; as if he needed time to collect his thoughts, he slapped at a mosquito that had landed on his shoulder, then took her by the hand. But what he did say was pure anticlimax. 'Got your soap?'

She stopped to get the tube of soap from her haversack and followed him out on to the ledge. The rock was slippery. She inched forward until the spray was striking her arm. It was cold. She gave a tiny shriek of dismay and tugged back on Finn's hand. 'It's freezing!'

He was standing full under the water, which had plastered his hair to his scalp and was running in rivulets down his chest. Raising his voice over the constant roar of the falls, he said, 'It's invigorating. Pass me the soap.'

He didn't look like a man eaten up by passion. She watched as he lathered his hair, the bubbles sliding down his ribs and hips in a way that secretly fascinated her.

Maybe she was the one who needed the cold shower, she thought. Not Finn.

Then he flicked his hair out of his eyes and passed her the tube of soap. 'Wash my back?'

Jenessa slathered her palms with soap. His skin felt cold as she smoothed the planes of his back and traced the long indentation of his spine to the taut buttocks. She didn't feel cold. She felt almost faint with desire.

He turned round and saw her face. Once again, Jenessa thought, he looked as though the ground had shifted beneath his feet, throwing him off balance. In silence he took the soap from her, squeezed some on his palms, then let his hands slide over her breasts, her waist and her hips; she swayed toward him and suddenly they were kissing each other with raw hunger, oblivious to the dancing white spray and the sunlight glinting off their wet, entwined bodies. When Finn finally released her, the pulse was racing at the base of his throat and Jenessa was shaking. 'You're cold,' he said hoarsely.

She shook her head, wordless. Stroking her rapt face, down which droplets of water trickled like tears, Finn muttered, 'We'd better go back... you should dry your hair.'

He had done nothing she hadn't wanted him to do, and he was saying, indirectly, that this episode was over. That they would put on their clothes, go back to the campsite and begin the normal routine of the day. Jenessa knew one thing with absolute certainty: she didn't want it to be over. Something that felt so right and so inevitable should continue to its natural conclusion; she was sure of that. But what if he didn't feel the same way? She said, 'Finn, do you want to make love to me?' and felt her heart slamming against her ribs as she waited for his reply.

He lifted her fingers to his mouth, kissing them one by one. 'I want that more than I've ever wanted anything in my life,' he said roughly. 'But——'

His face, as unguarded as she had ever seen it, looked as if he had just been given a gift that he hadn't anticipated receiving—a perfect gift of incomparable value. Touched to the heart, she said with attempted lightness, 'The tent would be more comfortable than here.'

'Are you sure about this?'

'More sure than I've ever been about anything.'

Afterwards she was never entirely clear how they got themselves and their clothes back to the campsite. Finn had wrapped her in a towel; she did remember that. And the first thing he did, after spreading his sleeping-bag flat so that it was big enough for both of them, was to rub her hair dry. She was kneeling beside him; when he had finished, he said soberly, 'Are you still sure, Jenessa?'

She took the towel from him and scrubbed at his scalp, her breasts bouncing; stroking a damp strand back from his forehead, she reached up and kissed him. Her lips were cool and touchingly inexperienced. But there was no mistaking the pleasure she took in the kiss, or her willingness to learn.

He drew her down on the sleeping-bag, throwing one thigh over hers as he gathered her into the circle of his arms. 'I want you always to remember the first time you made love,' he said quietly. 'There's no need to be frightened—I wouldn't hurt you for the world.'

He was in so many ways a stranger to her, this big man with the dark blue eyes, yet Jenessa knew she trusted his words implicitly. As she lay there beside him, she was aware of him setting himself to please her, watching her every response, listening for the catch in her breath, her first small moan of pleasure, doing nothing until he was sure she was ready for it; and all the while she herself was beginning to learn the feel, the weight, the generosity and the lightning-swift responses that were his essence. She lost all track of time and place; the only realities were the burning heat of Finn's body and the fierce impulsions of her own.

When he first let his fingers drift between her legs, playing with her until she shuddered with delight, she cried out his name in sheer wonderment, arching toward him in the oldest of invitations. She was as slick as if she were still immersed in the waterfall; he reached for the small foil packet beside the sleeping-bag, then guided himself into her, his weight on one elbow, his eyes watchful.

Jenessa gave a tiny gasp of pain, biting her lip, and felt him draw back. This whole experience was new to her; but she had sensed more than once the iron control Finn was exerting over his own responses the better to please her. She said strongly, 'Now, Finn—please,' and moved her hips beneath his with instinctive, if unpracticed skill.

He moved deeper and she saw his face convulse in that mingling of pain and pleasure that had been driving her further and further into the unknown ever since Finn had first lain beside her. To be filled by him suffused her with an elemental hunger so new to her and so overwhelming that she pulled him down on top of her, quivering like a too taut wire. His rhythms became her rhythms, drawing her closer and closer to the storm's heart. Letting go of everything but blind need, she felt the rhythms become her, gathering her and whirling her in a wild dance and then dropping her into the utter calm that was the very center.

But that was not all. From that calm she heard Finn's harsh, rapid breathing and heard her name flung from his lips as deep within her his body found its own release. He hung his head, gasping for air, his chest heaving. There was a sheen of sweat on his forehead, and it was that one small detail that filled Jenessa with a deep and abiding tenderness.

She put her arms round his shoulders. His heart was racing against her breast, and as he moved once more within her she held him as closely as she could. She had learned so much about him, she thought. He had given her the best that was in him; that she had been afraid of him earlier this morning now seemed absurd.

Perhaps making love was a way of discovering what a man was really like.

'Finn,' she whispered, her breath wafting his cheek, 'thank you...'

He raised his head. 'Are you all right?'

She gave a throaty chuckle. 'Very much so. And you?'

'Never better.'

As he levered some of his weight off her, she clutched him to her. 'Don't go... not yet.'

'I'd like to stay here forever,' Finn said; then his eyes widened as his words, with all their implications, struck home.

The tenderness she had felt shifted to an emotion more complex and compelling, an emotion as deep and mysterious as the pool at the foot of the waterfall. Finn was part of her now, Jenessa thought with a springing joy. They could never wholly be separated, no matter what happened.

She said in a rush, 'Do you know what this was like for me? It's as though we switched roles. You guided me into a new territory. You knew the way, I didn't. If you were in a hurry, I never knew it, and if perhaps there were places you might have wanted to go you held back if you thought I'd like other places better.' Her voice gathered strength. 'You made sure I didn't stumble over any rocks or fall off any cliffs. But, more than that, you showed me all the beauty there was to be seen as we traveled together. Such beauty as I couldn't have imagined.'

She had run out of words. His eyes, so close to hers, were like dark pools themselves; she had no idea what he was thinking. As he rubbed a hand across his forehead she saw, with another of those pangs of emotion that seemed to melt her soul into tenderness, that his fingers were not quite steady. He said in a voice new to her, 'I—thank you, Jenessa.' His mouth twisted. 'You have this knack for knocking me off balance.'

'I don't mean to,' Jenessa said in quick distress.

He ran a finger the length of her lower lip. 'It's okay.' Then he added with a faint smile that didn't quite reach his eyes, 'But I do have to move.'

As the heat of his body was lifted from hers, she felt bereft. Then he went outside, leaving her with emotions as tangled as a thicket of alders. What did this new tenderness mean? Was it love? Or gratitude? Or, more pragmatically, sexual satiation? She had no experience to fall back on, no guidelines in this land where she and a man had joined in the most intimate way possible.

She also felt, she realized, extremely hungry. Disconcerted that such an ordinary concern could occupy her, she pulled Finn's sleeping-bag around her for comfort.

The tent flap rustled and Finn crawled back in. Kneeling beside her, he said, 'It's nine-thirty. We should get going.'

'We should,' she groaned.

'I could bring you breakfast in bed.'

'That's certainly not in the guide handbook.' She didn't want to get going. She wanted to stay and make love the whole day through. But Finn had retreated from her in a way she couldn't have defined but that was, nevertheless, very real. 'One kiss, and I'll get up,' she added with lazy challenge.

He laughed. 'You know darn well if I kiss you that we'll be here all day. Coffee and oatmeal for breakfast?'

It was on the tip of her tongue to ask if it would be so terrible if they stayed all day. After all, he was the one who had said he would like to stay here forever. But her new vulnerability somehow precluded the question. She wasn't, she thought honestly, ready to be turned down. It would hurt too much.

Her lashes flickered as her thoughts carried her forward. Their lovemaking had been earth-shattering for her. But perhaps Finn, accustomed to more sophisticated partners, had been bored.

His fingers had been trembling; he couldn't have been bored.

Trembling fingers were a physical response and men were physical creatures.

'Tea and oatmeal for me,' Jenessa said with an artificial yawn. 'I'll be right out.'

Finn had put on a pair of jeans while he'd been outside. Deciding her nudity gave him an unfair advantage, Jenessa kept the sleeping-bag tucked under her chin and waited while he put on a clean shirt and found a pair of socks in his pack. The sight of his lean fingers—fingers that had drawn from her responses she hadn't known existed—pulling the wool sock over his foot filled her with a helpless yearning.

I'm not in love with him. I can't be. I couldn't have fallen in love just like that.

Scared that her face might give her away, she burrowed into his sleeping-bag, and caught from it the elusive scent of his body. I do love Finn, she thought. It's not logical and it doesn't make sense. But I do.

It was a relief when he left the tent to start a fire. She got dressed quickly, tidied up their gear and dragged it outside, and busied herself taking the tent down. She drank her tea and ate her oatmeal like a woman in a dream. But when Finn accidentally bumped into her as she was drying the dishes, the dream fell apart. She looked up at him, her green eyes liquid with emotion. He froze to the spot, still clutching her elbow. 'Jenessa, I—look, there's no easy way to say this. Don't confuse sex with love—there's a big difference.'

An abyss had opened at her feet. Jenessa croaked, 'You made love to me with feeling.'

'Yeah...but I'm not in love with you.'

'We made *love*,' she repeated desperately. 'How do I separate them?'

His face hardened. 'In ten days I'll be gone from here. Off to Venezuela. And you've got a film crew you're responsible for, and all your other commitments. Our lives will part—they have to. I wouldn't have touched you if I'd thought you hadn't understood that.'

Ruthless, she thought with a shiver. But how could such ruthlessness coexist with the sensitivity with which Finn had initiated her into the act of love?

Perhaps the act of love had truly been an act.

'You can't have intimacy without feelings,' she cried, and wondered whom she was trying to convince, Finn or herself.

'They're feelings of the moment,' Finn said.

'They don't last?'

'They're real at the time. That doesn't mean they have to go on forever.'

'I hate this conversation,' Jenessa said in a low voice.

'Then we'd better get moving... you said we had a long way to go today.'

'Now who's running?' she demanded, and began shoving the dishes in the Duluth pack.

Finn didn't answer. Not that she had expected him to.

She had learned something else by making love with Finn, she thought unhappily: that he didn't love her.

CHAPTER TEN

JENESSA'S predictions when she had first woken that morning turned out to be all too accurate. It was a hot, windless day and the flies—including the voracious stouts—were out in droves. Despite that, she and Finn made good time. They portaged up the side of the waterfall, neither one of them referring to what had happened there; they travelled a chain of three lakes, their blades slicing the water in such perfect unison that the canoe moved swiftly over the sparkling blue water. They ate lunch as they went and talked almost not at all. Which gave Jenessa far too much time to think.

They reached the campsite well before sunset. She had been there twice with her father and Ryan, and it had changed very little. The lake was still edged by tall grasses that rustled in the slightest breeze; flocks of black ducks and green-winged teal burst into the air at their approach, wings whickering. Trout were jumping for flies, leaving little circles of ripples on the placid water. As soon as they had landed, Jenessa said, 'I'm going to see if I can catch our supper.'

Finn nodded. 'I'll set up the tent and look for wood.'

She landed two fine speckled trout in short order. Finn then stripped to his shorts and dived into the lake, and as she cleaned the fish she watched him swim to the nearest island and back, his body slicing through the water with precision and fierce energy.

The energy of sexual frustration because he knew he wasn't going to make love with her again? Or the energy of remorse that he had?

Mixing tea-biscuit dough with absent-minded skill, she wondered why, if she'd waited until the age of nearly twenty-six to fall in love, she'd chosen a man as difficult and inaccessible as Finn. The main reason she'd gone out with Mac had been his suitability: the same occupation and skills and background. But she'd never been in any danger of falling in love with Mac. Oh, no, she'd waited for Finn Marston, who lived anywhere from Indonesia to Venezuela and didn't want anything to do with love and marriage.

Finn waded into shore, flipping his wet hair out of his eyes and hitching at the waistband of his shorts. Her flour-coated hands went slack. She must be in love: she was hurting too much for it to be anything else.

By the time he'd dressed and hung up his wet towel, Jenessa was preparing wild rice to go with the trout fillets. 'Supper will be half an hour,' she said. 'If you walk along the shore, you might see the river otters—they have tunnels in the bank further down.'

'Okay, I'll do that.'

She couldn't bear him near her and she was furious with him for leaving. How's that for logic? she thought pettishly, putting the pot of rice on to boil and reaching for the axe to split more wood.

Forty-five minutes later the fillets were fried to a pink, crisp perfection, the tea biscuits had risen lightly in the pan and the rice was steaming in the pot. Finn, however, hadn't come back. It had been a very long day for Jenessa, beginning in bliss and plummeting to misery, and briefly she contemplated eating without him. But then her training reasserted itself. Finn wouldn't alarm her by purposely being late. Perhaps he was absorbed in watching the otters and had forgotten the time.

She carefully pushed the frying pan to the edge of the grill and headed out along the shore. The sky was ribbed with gold and apricot; the trees were gathering the darkness into themselves. A pair of loons wailed back and forth behind the island, their eerie cries the very voice of the wilderness. If she shouted Finn's name, she might frighten them; sure-footed, she followed an old moose trail along the lake's edge, longing for the tranquility that such beauty normally brought her.

As she reached an untidy clump of spruce trees that had been saplings the last time she saw them, she sighted the otters swimming offshore, leaving V-shaped wakes on water daubed with gold and apricot and palest blue. Although they were big, thickset animals, they wove above and below the surface with a sleek, sinuous grace. They looked absolutely at home, she thought. It was hard not to believe that they were happy.

To her consternation Jenessa realized she was crying, slow tears that hung on her lashes and crept down her cheeks. Until yesterday she had been like the otters, doing what was most natural to her in an environment that was home. But yesterday had fractured all that she had previously taken for granted.

A twig snapped and the spruce branches rustled as someone pushed against them. It was, of course, Finn. He had been walking hard along the trail and barely stopped himself from cannoning into her. He was being so careful not to touch her, she thought bitterly, and dashed at her eyes. 'Supper's ready,' she said, and stared straight at him, refusing to acknowledge her tears.

A muscle twitched in his jaw. 'I was watching the otters and forgot the time,' he said formally.

They marched back to the camp in single file. The trout fillets were delicious. Gazing into the flames,

Jenessa remembered the five-pound trout her father had caught the last time they were here; Ryan had fried it in a crunchy whole-wheat batter and had told them tall tales about bears as the fire had died to a pit of glowing embers . . . scarcely an hour after she'd gone to bed she'd had a lurid nightmare about being torn to pieces by a huge black bear.

It was dark by the time they'd eaten. Jenessa lit the propane lamp and said tersely, 'I'll clean up.' Finn took out a book—a technical manual to do with oil rigs, she noticed; no novels for Finn—and propped himself up to read. When she'd finished the dishes, she wandered down to the shore. The clustered stars looked cold and distant, the thin sliver of moon false in its promise.

The temperature was dropping fast and the air struck chill on her face. She walked back toward the fire, picked up her book and tried to concentrate on intrigues and emotions that meant nothing to her. Finally Finn stood up. 'I'm going to call it a day,' he said.

'I want to finish this chapter,' Jenessa replied with complete untruth, not looking up.

She sensed him watching her. Every nerve in her body screaming with tension, she flipped a page. Then he turned away, took off his boots in the vestibule of the tent and crawled inside. She wasn't going anywhere near that tent until he was asleep, she decided grimly, and added another log to the fire, watching the sparks whirl up into the darkness, wishing she were ten years old again, wishing she were anywhere but where she was.

The log burned down; she added another and then another. The moon climbed in the sky. A horned owl barked on the other side of the lake, and from the faraway hills a second owl answered it. Although Jenessa was tired and craved sleep, her nerves were twitching and the thought of lying in the tent listening to Finn's slow breathing was more than she could contemplate.

She drifted into a daze, almost hypnotized by the throbbing orange heart of the fire. Her head fell forward to her chest. Jerking herself upright, she thought, This is crazy; I can't stay up all night... and heard, from the tent, a man's voice cry out in anguish, 'No...*no*!'

The hairs rose on the back of her neck. It was Finn; he was dreaming. She rose and took two quick steps toward the tent. Then, although it went against every instinct in her body, she retreated and sank back on the rock again. Finn didn't want her help. Didn't want it or need it. He had made that all too clear.

She thrust a log on to the fire. As the flames caught at it greedily, Finn blundered out of the tent, blinking in the orange light.

He was naked save for his briefs, and for a moment, at the sight of her, naked shock showed in his face. In a voice raspy with sleep he demanded, 'What are you doing up? I thought you were asleep.'

'I've been reading.' In open challenge Jenessa added, 'You had a bad dream.'

A shudder ran through his body. Wanting him, hating him, yearning to comfort him, she placed another chunk of birch in the middle of the flames and said, 'Why don't you put some clothes on, Finn, and then tell me about it? It's pretty hard to pretend nothing's wrong when for two weeks we're sharing the same sleeping place.'

Congratulations, Jenessa, she thought drily, you didn't say we're sleeping together. She watched as Finn crossed barefooted to the fire and crouched down beside her. 'Why, Jenessa?' he said with dangerous quietness. 'Why do you want to know?'

She blanked out the almost overwhelming need to put her hand on his shoulder. 'That's twice you've woken with a nightmare. When I was little if I had a bad dream I'd tell my dad about it, and it never seemed quite so scary afterwards.'

'I have trouble seeing you as a father substitute.'

'Red herring, Finn.'

'You're so right.' He glowered at her. 'So who do you talk to now when you have a nightmare?'

'No one...can you imagine Ryan doling out sympathy because you had a bad dream?'

In spite of himself Finn smiled, the firelight glancing over his face. 'Not really... I'll be right back.'

She put a pot of water on to boil and gathered the makings for tea. Finn came back out, shoving his shirt into his waistband. Without meeting her eyes, he sat down next to her, took a deep breath and said rapidly, 'Three years ago a young fellow came to work for me—Jim Butler. I liked him from the start. He was intelligent and strong and he had that sixth sense that's invaluable but that you can't instill in people who don't have it.' His voice slowed. 'We don't have big crews at blowouts, and you spend a lot of time together...I—I guess Jim became the kid brother I never had.'

Lost in memory, he gazed into the fire. 'We were working in horrendous conditions at a gas-well blowout last April—it had been out of control for nearly a month. Gasoline everywhere, one spark and the whole thing would have gone sky-high. Deafening noise. Freezing temperatures. And hydrogen sulfide gas that's lethal over seven hundred parts per million.' He shifted on the rock. 'Jim inhaled the hydrogen sulfide. Died instantly.'

'I'm so sorry…' Jenessa said helplessly, wishing she were wiser, searching for something to say that wouldn't sound banal.

'It should have been me. Not him.'

Shocked, she blurted, 'How can you say that?'

As if he were explaining the obvious, Finn said, 'He was a lot younger. He had a girlfriend. He had all kinds of possibilities ahead of him.'

Like a hunter who knew the prey was round the next bend in the trail, Jenessa was acutely aware of being very close to the mystery that was Finn. Treading carefully, she said, 'There's nothing ahead for you?'

'I've already told you I'm not into love and marriage and raising kids,' he said impatiently.

'You haven't told me why, though.'

Lifting the lid from the pot of boiling water, Finn threw two tea bags in. 'In the dream I know what's going to happen to him, and I'm trying to get to him to warn him. But he can't hear me over the noise, and my boots are mired in mud and gas so I keep slipping and falling….' His smile was mirthless. 'If I'm lucky, I wake up then. If not, I see him fall and I know I'm too late.'

Forgetting all that had happened in the last twenty-four hours, Jenessa rested her hand on Finn's wrist with the simple desire to comfort him. 'I'm sorry Jim's dead. But it wasn't your fault.'

With his other hand he traced a blue vein across the back of her hand. 'It should have been me,' he repeated.

Everything that Jenessa's life had stood for negated that statement. She said, speaking from a depth she hadn't known she possessed, 'Come to bed with me, Finn. Now.'

His eyes, dark as night, seemed to look straight into her soul. 'Because we're alive and he's dead…'

'I wish we could change that—but we can't.' She bit her lip, feeling his wrist warm beneath her fingers. 'I can't explain it; I don't have the words. It's not the time for words—I just want to be close to you.'

He stood up, pulling her to her feet. Smoke swirled around them. The owl hooted, closer this time, and the river grasses whispered secretively in the darkness. Keeping one of her hands clasped in his, Finn led her to the tent.

He spread his sleeping-bag flat. Then they fell on each other, discarding their clothes with frantic haste until bare flesh lay against bare flesh, warmth against warmth, pulse against pulse, in an affirmation of all it meant to be alive.

That was how it began for Jenessa. But this was Finn whose body was wrapped around hers, whom—wisely or unwisely—she loved. With innate generosity, and calling upon everything she had learned from him the first time they had made love, she opened to him as if she were one of the water lilies whose petals spread to the sun. With her lips and hands she roamed his body with a freedom that last time she had been too shy to claim. Made even bolder by the dim, flickering light from the fire, she grasped the throbbing center of his maleness, then straddled him and let herself be impaled upon it. As she leaned forward, achingly aware of the ecstasy of being filled by him, he took her breasts in his hands, stroking them until waves of pleasure broke over her. Then, taking her by the hips, he moved strongly within her.

It was a fierce and primitive lovemaking, without words or the need for them. Jenessa matched him gift for gift and demand for demand, and when their rhythms fused into a single wave that tumbled and broke on the shore she knew that that synchronicity had been inevitable from the start.

The harsh panting she could hear was her own. Her own and Finn's, joined. She curved over his body, collapsing on top of him, and as his arms wrapped around her, holding her close, she gave a deep sigh of repletion. Within seconds she was asleep. And if Finn stayed awake, warmed by her weight as he stared up at the roof of the tent, she never knew that.

Daylight came soon. Too soon for Jenessa. She lay still, feeling Finn's breath stir her hair. Her back was curled into his chest and she wanted to stay there forever. Although he was sound asleep, she realized with inward amusement that he was very ready to ravish her. Which would not, she admitted to herself, be at all against her wishes.

At some point in the night he had taken her sleeping-bag and spread it over the two of them. She pulled it up to her chin. She didn't want Finn to wake up. Would he regret what they had done? Would he push her away, as he had yesterday? She could wait for those answers, she thought, and let her lashes drift to her cheeks.

It seemed only minutes later that Finn stirred beside her and Jenessa was awake again. But by the look of the sun at least an hour had passed. She stretched with lazy grace, lay back against his chest and looked over her shoulder at him. 'Good morning.'

He said quizzically, 'You look very pleased with yourself.'

She loved the rasp of his body hair against her bare back. 'I could get used to this,' she said with an impudent grin. 'What's for breakfast?'

'Let's call Room Service.'

'I'll have fresh papaya juice with almond croissants and Colombian coffee,' she said promptly. 'Lots of whipped cream on the coffee.'

'No strawberries in champagne? No omelet with fresh chanterelles? Come on, Jenessa, live a little.'

She loved it when he laughed. Twisting to face him, she said with mock-sternness, 'You need a shave.'

'You talk too much,' he growled, and closed her mouth with a kiss.

It was a very comprehensive kiss. Catching her breath, Jenessa murmured, 'Add eggs hollandaise.'

'Don't like 'em.' In the same voice he added, 'Do you have any idea what we're doing here?'

'Enjoying ourselves?' she suggested, running her fingers down his ribs.

'Apart from that, Jenessa,' he said wryly.

'No. But maybe we shouldn't worry about it right now. Maybe we should just go with what feels right.'

Capturing her hand, he said, 'If we do that, we'll be here all day.'

She said pertly, 'Sounds good to me.'

He buried his face in the soft line of her throat. 'I might be every kind of a fool, but I think we should get on our way. I need to get to the summer house, Jenessa; it's important to me.'

'So there's a reason you're so impatient,' Jenessa said thoughtfully. 'It's not just that you're a typical businessman who's always in a hurry.'

'Right,' he said with a touch of irony. 'Although I'm that, too.'

'I noticed.'

'Sometimes you notice too much.'

'I've noticed that your ribs look better,' she remarked.

He lifted his head. 'I didn't tell you the whole story last night...there was a sequel to Jim's death.' Playing with the hem of the sleeping-bag, he went on, 'I went to his funeral, did everything I could for his family—then I went back to work. Indonesia this time. Heat and humidity like you wouldn't believe, and all kinds of technical hitches. But I couldn't get him off my mind. So I got careless—made a mistake I'd have fired anyone else for and that could have had disastrous results. Luckily I was the only one who got hurt. But it sure put a scare in me... Jonah, who's my second-in-command and who's been with me for years, told me flat out that I'd better take some time off. When Jonah talks that way, I listen. Which is why I came to Newfoundland in the first place.'

'You told me you hadn't had a holiday for five years...'

'I haven't had a proper break in the last ten—since I started the company. It's a competitive field and I wanted my company to be one of the best.' He shrugged. 'I've wondered in the past few weeks if I shouldn't take more of an administrative role and leave Jonah in control of the field work; he's very capable. But I'd probably miss the excitement.'

'The edge of danger,' Jenessa said shrewdly.

'There's nothing like the silence that falls when you cap a blowout,' Finn said. 'It's tremendously satisfying work, and yeah, it's dangerous. But there are dangers in what you do, Jenessa. I watched you go down the rapids. And you could be in bad trouble if you walked headlong into a bear.'

'I surprised one once,' she confessed. 'I was alone, too. This bear and I stared at each other for what was probably five seconds and felt like a lifetime. It took two steps toward me, sniffed the air, then shuffled off the other way. But it's only happened once in all the years I've been in the woods.'

'We both love our jobs,' he said.

His words hung in the air. Don't get attached to me, was that the warning? she wondered. Or was it a simple statement of fact and she was being overly sensitive? She said, 'I wouldn't give up mine for anything.'

His lashes flickered. Starting to pull on his clothes, he said, 'Why are my jeans in one corner and my socks in another?'

He was deliberately side-stepping the challenge she had thrown at him. 'Because we were both in a hurry last night,' Jenessa said, her voice muffled as she pulled her sweatshirt over her head.

'I didn't dream some of the things you did to me?'

'Describe them and I'll tell you,' she replied naughtily.

Finn chuckled. 'I might embarrass both of us.' Then, as he reached into his pack for a clean T-shirt, he added in another voice altogether, 'My God, Jenessa—we were in so much of a hurry last night, I didn't take any precautions. How in hell could I have forgotten? I've never done that before.'

She didn't want to be reminded that there had been other women in his life. Sounding artificial even to her own ears, she said, 'I didn't even think about it.'

'Then you'd better start—the last thing I need is a pregnant woman on my hands.'

Suddenly furious, she said, 'You don't have to worry on my account. If I get pregnant, I'll look after myself. And the baby.'

Her cheekbones were flushed with anger. He took in the brilliant green of her eyes and the slim length of her legs as she yanked on her bush pants. 'Ryan notwithstanding,' he said, 'I suspect you've often had to look after yourself.'

'Don't you go feeling sorry for me. Where the *devil* are my socks?'

'By my pillow,' Finn said blandly, passing them to her. 'How did they get there, Jenessa?'

She could remember in graphic detail exactly how they got there. Scarlet-cheeked, she snatched them from him and mumbled, 'Go make strawberries in champagne. Or slice the papaya. Just get out of my hair!'

He tweaked a strand of it, openly laughing at her. 'I can't imagine being bored with you,' he said. 'Would you be satisfied with oatmeal?'

Letting her eyes wander the length of his body, she said sweetly, 'The longer I spend with you, the more exotic my tastes are becoming. Oatmeal seems pretty boring.'

'At the risk of sounding conceited, I could give you something that wouldn't bore you. But you'll have to wait until tonight.' He grinned at her, backing out of the tent. 'In the meantime I'll add raisins and apple to the oatmeal.'

Jenessa, left alone, discovered that paramount among the ferment of emotions in her breast was happiness. She brushed her hair, took out her toothbrush and toothpaste and went outside.

CHAPTER ELEVEN

IT SEEMED as though nature had conspired to give Jenessa and Finn a perfect day. The sun shone from a cloudless sky, the breeze was just enough to keep the flies away, and they saw two moose, five caribou and a pair of golden eagles. Their campsite was on a small island with a white, sandy beach. They swam, they made love before supper and again when they went to bed, and as Jenessa drifted off to sleep in the circle of Finn's arms she realized she had never known before what perfect happiness was.

She woke at dawn. Finn had turned away from her in the night; she rested her cheek against the smooth plane of his back and felt a knot of tension in the pit of her stomach. She knew exactly why it was there.

Their campsite tonight was less than two miles from her father's log house, the house where she had lived until she was thirteen. She wanted to camp early enough so that she could go and see it. Was she going to tell Finn her plan? Did she want him to go with her? Or was she better to go on her own?

The solidity and warmth of Finn's back seemed to mock her. Yes, he and she had made love and fallen asleep in each other's arms, but they had not once talked about their feelings for each other as they'd lain together; in the act of love they had exchanged no words of love. And why did she keep hoping that they would? For Finn their affair was very much one of the moment. He had told her as much.

If she shared the visit to her father's house with him, she was revealing a huge part of herself. And for what? With the unspoken wish that he would do the same?

He had taken—and she was beginning to hate the word—precautions last night. Why was he so dead-set against falling in love? Could it be anything at all to do with his impatience to get to the summer house where his mother had died?

Too many questions, she realized, and not enough answers. Easing her body away from Finn's, she gathered up her clothes, not bothering with a swimsuit, and hurried down to the lake to have a swim. Clouds dappled the sky and the wind had shifted; there would be rain before evening. She swam back and forth for perhaps ten minutes, churning up the water in a futile effort to dissolve the tension in her belly, then headed for the shore.

Finn was standing at the lake's edge with one hand braced against the truck of a silver birch, watching her. Although the knot in her stomach tightened at the sight of him, she looked outwardly composed as she picked her way among the rocks and bent for her towel.

Droplets of water trickled down her body. He said harshly. 'I know you so well and yet I know nothing about you.'

'I don't think you want to.'

'It's better that I don't!' he said violently. 'Better for both of us, Jenessa.'

So she had her answer. She would go alone to the log house because Finn didn't want any more of her than he already had. She said coolly, 'I'd really prefer that you not speak for me, Finn,' and started pulling on her clothes over her damp skin.

'You never let up, do you?' he said unpleasantly.

Yesterday she'd been convinced that such perfect happiness by its very nature had to last. She'd been a fool. 'Do we have to start the day off by fighting?' she blazed. She hauled her sweater over her head and stalked past him, her wet towel dangling from her hand.

His answer was to swing her round by the elbow and kiss her full on the lips. As his mouth moved against hers his rage and hunger were clearly to be read, but beneath them Jenessa would have sworn there was desperation. She pulled free, not wanting that knowledge. If he was to be the enemy, then let him be that and nothing else. She couldn't cope with his ambivalence any more than she could handle her own seesawing emotions.

Loathing how petty she sounded, she snapped, 'I do wish you'd shave before you kiss me,' and marched toward the tent.

She made blueberry bannock for breakfast, along with slices of fresh orange and steaming hot coffee. As they sat on opposite sides of the campfire, Finn ate in silence, although it was the silence of thought rather than of anger. Adding sugar to his mug, he said unexpectedly, 'Do you know what I like about you?'

Jenessa nearly choked on her coffee. Suppressing a reply that verged on the obscene, she muttered, 'I can't imagine.'

'You don't give up. You don't dissolve into tears when I'm angry, or pretend you're feeling fine when you're feeling lousy. And you're a real fighter—you give as good as you get; I like that.' His smile was crooked. 'Plus, of course, you're a superlative cook.'

'Why do we have to fight at all?' she burst out.

'When I figure out the answer to that one, I'll let you know. Want some more coffee?'

She held out her mug. If she were a fighter, wouldn't she invite Finn to go to her father's house with her? 'There's more bannock,' she said politely. 'It won't keep.'

They were on the water by nine, and at eleven-thirty it started to rain. They put on their rain gear, snacked on cheese and crackers and kept paddling. A stillwater led into the next lake. Along its meandering shores purple asters and golden rod were massed among the fluffy pink flowers of pye weed; lily pads scraped the underside of the canoe. Because the water was shallow and they were traveling slowly, they surprised a beaver swimming toward its lodge of piled saplings; the warning slap of its tail was like the crack of a bullet. Around the next bend ducklings were peeping in the reeds as raindrops splashed an accompaniment on the water.

The second lake was six miles long and the wind had freshened. Jenessa was pink-cheeked with exertion by the time they reached the far end, where she planned to camp. The meadows that had been there thirteen years ago were now dotted with delicate young junipers and squat spruce trees; when she finally found a flat area where they could anchor the tarp, impatience was tugging at her nerves.

Because they had eaten very little lunch, she had an excuse for an early supper. She reconstituted a package of dried stroganoff, with apple pancakes for dessert; as soon as they had eaten, she said to Finn, 'Do you mind cleaning up? I need to stretch my legs... That's the trouble with canoeing—great for the biceps but no good for the hamstrings.'

While she'd tried very hard to sound casual, she wasn't at all sure she'd succeeded; she should have made a habit of going for an evening walk, she thought, angry with herself for not planning more adequately in advance.

Finn shot her a keen glance. 'You exercised this morning when you swam.'

Cursing herself for taking that swim, Jenessa answered lightly, 'A big part of my job is keeping fit. I won't be that long, okay?'

Taking his silence for consent, she got up, pulled on her rain jacket and walked purposely away from the camp through the juniper trees. Fortunately the rain had let up a little, otherwise he might have been even more suspicious of her sudden desire for exercise. As the taller trees enveloped her, she risked a quick look back over her shoulder. Finn was still sitting by the fire, his hands cupping his mug, his gaze trained on her. She gave a little wave, moved out of sight and lengthened her stride. It was a four-mile round trip and she wanted to spend some time at the house when she got there.

Rain hung like teardrops on the plumed boughs of the junipers, and the springy branches of lambkill whipped at her knees. The animal trail she was following wasn't the most direct route to the cove where she had lived, but it was easier than ploughing through the undergrowth. Occasionally taking out her compass to check her bearings, she strode on. The knot in her stomach now felt as big as a boulder. She shouldn't have eaten so much stroganoff. But her appetite was normally good, and Finn would have wondered if she'd only picked at her food.

A robin flew away in a whirr of wings. A whiskeyjack screamed at her from the top of a birch tree. She came to the big rock where she had often dreamed away a summer afternoon as a child, then among the pointed spruce trees on the horizon saw the tall, twisted trunk of the dead pine that stood only a hundred feet from her father's log house. Her heartbeat quickened; picking up speed, she darted along the trail. To her ears came the burble of the brook that circled the pine before it emptied into the cove. The brook had long been one of her imaginary playmates, for she had grown up without the company of other children.

Where there had once been a cleared path along the brook there was now a tangle of alders. Not caring how much noise she made, Jenessa pushed her way through it. The brook itself hadn't changed; with a leap of recognition she saw the moss-covered rock where warty brown toads had always lived, and below it the pool where once she had surprised a cow moose with her day-old calf.

The brook spread itself over the stones on the shoreline of the cove. The lake hadn't changed either, she thought. The islands were the same, one shaped like the rounded back of an otter, the other blunt-nosed as a turtle. The chain of black rocks where she had learned to swim was the same as well.

Almost with reluctance her eyes traveled along the line of rocks toward the sweep of sandy beach above which her father had built his house. She wanted to see smoke rising from the chimney, she thought with painful truth. She wanted to hear the ring of her father's axe in the woodpile and the echo of her own voice calling him in for dinner. She wanted that to be the same, too.

Her brow furrowed in puzzlement. She couldn't see the house. Had the trees grown so much that it was hidden from view? They must have, although years ago her father had cut down all the maples that had restricted his view of the lake. She started running along the shore, her boots skidding on the slippery stones then sinking in the sand, and the thud of her heart in her ears was like the thud of a dull axe on wet wood.

She was closer now. The mossy roof, the stone chimney, the rounded logs so neatly notched at the corners... none of them was there. Frantically she clambered up the bank between the two junipers that she had planted when she was seven—and stopped dead.

The house had been burned to the ground.

With a whimper of disbelief she saw charred, rotting logs lying end over end; a few still clung to the corner posts, light shining through their mangled ribs. She crept closer. There, split by the heat, was the blackened doorframe; shattered glass from the windows lay in diamond-shaped pieces among the logs. Only the chimney, built of rock, stood intact.

Lightning... the house had been struck by lightning.

Then, like a blow to the chest, she realized what was missing. There was no sign of any of the furniture, of the books that had lined the walls, of the bone china that had been her mother's and that had been kept in the tall armoire in the corner by the chimney.

They had been taken away, she thought sickly. Stolen.

The fire hadn't been caused by lightning. It had been set.

Other details forced themselves upon her. Grass, tall and rank, swathed the ruined wood and thrust its way between the scorched floorboards. Alder bushes were flourishing among the fallen logs. Nature was reclaiming its own, she realized with a stab of agony. In a few more years there would be nothing to show that a man and his daughter had lived here for thirteen years.

From behind her she heard the sound of footsteps. Her throat closed in terror. If she turned around she would see the ghost of her father, come back to the cove now there was someone to share the scene of so much desecration...

'Jenessa,' Finn said, 'it's me; don't be afraid.'

A real man. Not a supernatural visitation. A real man, who she had more reason than most to know was made of flesh and blood. In a flash Jenessa's terror was usurped by an upsurge of such rage that, again, she was frightened. Tamping the rage down, she turned around. Finn was standing thirty feet away from her, his hands in his jacket pockets, his gaze intent on her face.

Feeling naked to him in a way that was new to her, and that she abhorred, she said tightly, 'What are you doing here?'

'I followed you.'

'I see that. I want to know why.'

'Because, for the first time since we've met, I thought you were deliberately lying to me. I wanted to know why.'

'I lied to you because I didn't want you here. I would have thought that was obvious.'

He walked closer, his boots crunching in the coarse sand. 'Whose house was this?'

'Mine, of course—and my father's. Didn't you guess that?'

'I wondered.'

'Now that you've satisfied your curiosity you can go back to the camp. Where you belong.'

With one hand he indicated the heap of wreckage that had once been a home. 'Who burned it down?'

Her nails dug into her palms. It was the question that had hovered on the edge of her consciousness ever since she had seen the first signs of the damage, but the answer had never been an issue. 'Your grandfather,' she said. 'Who else?'

'This is his land,' Finn said evenly. 'Why would he destroy someone's house?'

In a staccato voice she replied, 'It became his land when I was thirteen—he stole it from my father. Who died of a heart attack as a result. Perhaps your beloved late grandfather didn't want the evidence of what he'd done to remain standing. I'm quite sure he didn't raze the house to the ground out of remorse.'

'You hate him.'

She nodded, her eyes as hard as glass. 'If ever I've hated anyone in my life, it's George Hilchey.'

Later she was to remember how Finn made no attempt to argue his grandfather's innocence. In a tone devoid of emotion he asked, 'How much land did your father own?'

'Nearly seven hundred acres. It nicely rounds off the parcel that was your grandfather's.' She almost spat the words at him. 'That you now own.'

'You didn't know the house had been destroyed.'

For a horrible moment Jenessa thought she was going to lose her control and weep in front of him. Steeling herself against both pain and tears, she said, 'I haven't been here for nearly thirteen years. No, I didn't know.'

'I'm sorry you had to find it like this,' Finn said.

She didn't want his sympathy any more than she wanted his presence here. And not for anything was she going to tell him that she'd come here hoping to take away one or two of her father's favorite books.

'How did my grandfather get the land?'

She swallowed, trying to ease the tightness in her throat. 'My father collected rare books and maps—it was his passion. My mother died when I was born, and I suppose that was where he put all his energy...into that, and bringing me up.' She bit her lip. 'Your grandfather offered my father an extremely rare edition of some old French maps of Newfoundland. It was a prize, the pearl for which one sells all the other pearls. But my father couldn't afford it. So your grandfather loaned him the money, a long-term loan, he said, and my father could gradually sell off some of his other books to pay him.'

Her voice had wavered. Finn said flatly, 'So I suppose my grandfather foreclosed.'

She nodded. 'My father was shocked, because he'd trusted your grandfather's word... Now that I'm an adult, I realize he was naïve about the ways of the world after living for so long away from it. Anyway, he and I set off in the canoe to go to Gander... he knew he could contact any number of dealers who'd buy the maps from him so he could pay off the loan. That evening he locked the maps in Ryan's old truck when we went inside a restaurant to eat and use the phone. When we came outside someone had broken the window and stolen them. My father knew what the loss of those maps meant—the loss of everything he held dear. He had a heart attack...Ryan and the ambulance drivers couldn't revive him.'

He had fallen, she remembered with another stab of pain, as a tall tree fell to the killing blow of the axe—slowly and irrevocably and with utter finality. No repair possible, no going back to the way things were.

Finn's voice broke into her thoughts. 'You believe my grandfather stole the maps.'

'Oh, yes. I have no proof. But who else would know enough to take a brown paper package from an old Ford truck?'

'And what happened to you after that, Jenessa?'

She said briefly, 'I was sent to live with my father's sister in Corner Brook. I wanted to live with Ryan—but the authorities didn't think it was fitting for a thirteen-year-old girl to be living with a bachelor who in those days was something of a reprobate.'

'What was she like?'

'Aunt Gladys? She didn't want me. And for the first time in my life I had to go to school. I didn't have a clue how to dress or what to say or how to behave...and, because I'd always had the free rein of my father's bookshelves, I knew far more about some things than the other kids, and absolutely nothing about the things that counted: pop stars and television and how to flirt.' Lost in the past, Jenessa made a helpless gesture. 'They were the three worst years of my life. Once I turned sixteen I left Aunt Gladys and went to live with Ryan.'

'It's a credit to you that you survived an upbringing like that—isolated with your father and then thrust as an adolescent into a totally hostile environment. No wonder you were out of touch with your sexuality.'

'I was terrified of the boys at school—they used to gang up on me because I was different. I was always a fighter, but I was no match for six or seven boys all bigger than me.'

A raindrop plopped on her nose. With a tiny shock she came back to the present, to the man with the dark blue eyes who was both her lover and the owner of all that once she had loved. 'I hardly ever talk about those three years,' she said dismissively. 'What's the point?'

'Exorcism,' Finn said bluntly. 'Did they rape you, those boys?'

'Oh, no.' Jenessa scuffed at the grass with her boot. 'But they used to laugh at my clothes and make fun of my figure, and sometimes they'd touch me in ways that made me feel dirty all over...so I suppose I grew up thinking I wasn't much good as a woman. That in some fundamental way I didn't fit.'

Had she been looking at Finn she might have realized something: that, while there was genuine compassion in his face, behind it he was thinking furiously. 'You loved your father,' he said. 'And he loved you.'

She nodded, digging at the roots with her heel. 'I never knew my mother so I never really missed her. My father wasn't a man to verbalize his feelings but I'm sure he loved me... I was lucky that way. I was free to roam the woods and ask him anything I needed to know... Not many children grow up with such freedom.'

'So that's why you know the area so well.'

'We camped at every one of the sites where you and I have stayed.'

'You love the land—the whole area we've covered.'

Surprised that Finn even needed to say this, she glanced up. 'I grew up feeling as though all of it was mine. I knew it. I understood it. Of course I loved it.'

'And you still do.'

Too befuddled by all the emotions she had gone through in the last half-hour to have any idea where he was headed, Jenessa nodded again. 'More than ever, I guess. Because now I realise how vulnerable it is to what we call progress.'

As if that was all he had needed, Finn said in a voice as sharp-edged as slate, 'That's why you were so anxious to guide me here, isn't it? Because you want the land and I'm the one who owns it now. Get to me and you've got the land.'

His words struck her as hard as if the rain had suddenly changed to pellets of ice. 'Of course not! That's nothing——'

Finn's lips thinned into a ferocious smile. 'That's why you made love to me.'

'It is *not*! For heaven's sake, Finn——'

She might just as well not have spoken. 'It all fits together so neatly,' he grated. 'You've got two weeks to make me see the land the way you do, two weeks to seduce me. Seduce me in more ways than one. So you make love to me by a waterfall so beautiful that I couldn't possibly be crass enough to allow it to be dammed. In the name of progress, to use your words.' He paled, his fists clenched at his sides. 'But there's more, isn't there, Jenessa? You didn't anticipate I'd do anything as practical as going to the drugstore. But I did. So the night I told you about Jim you made sure we were in such a hurry that birth control was the last thing on my mind. You might be pregnant right now, mightn't you? Is that what you're hoping? So that then I'll marry you and you'll really own the land? Is that what you were aiming for, Jenessa?'

Battered by words that had a horrible logic and were totally untrue, Jenessa said incoherently, 'No, I never thought that... you're twisting everything; it was never that way.'

'And to think that I was nearly taken in by you. By your big green eyes and your beautiful body.' He gave her a look of searing contempt. 'I thought you were honest. I thought I could trust that honesty. I sure let my hormones get in the way of my brains, didn't I? You've manipulated me from beginning to end.'

Her nails digging into her palms, Jenessa threw all her energy into one last attempt to stave off a nightmare worse than any she had ever dreamed. 'What you're saying simply isn't true,' she said unsteadily. 'I'm the woman you've slept with, Finn—I made love to you because I wanted *you*. For yourself. It was nothing to do with the land.'

'I don't believe you,' he said.

Two ravens croaked at each other from the trees, then flapped their way across the cove. Birds as black as the sodden beams of her father's house. As black as Finn was painting her… A little while ago Jenessa had thought the discovery of the ruined house was more than she could bear; she now discovered that pain could encompass every cell of her body, immobilizing her in its clutches. Her brain struggled for words to repudiate all Finn had said, but her heart was crying out another message, one devoid of hope. She said in the dead voice of despair, 'I can't argue with you any more—I won't. There's no point. If you can think that of me, believe that I could act that way, how could I convince you otherwise, just with words?'

'You can't—because actions speak louder than words.'

She had had enough. More than enough. Her nails digging into her fists, she muttered, 'Go back to the camp, Finn. I need to be by myself for a while.'

'So do I—believe me,' he said with savage emphasis. 'We'll get to the summer house tomorrow. After that I want to head back to Mac's lodge as fast as we can. I don't care where we camp or how tired we get—all I want is to see the last of you.'

Even before Finn had disappeared among the trees, tears were blurring Jenessa's vision. She let them slide down her cheeks, where they mingled with the rain. Moving as stiffly as an old woman, she sat down on one of the charred logs and closed her eyes.

CHAPTER TWELVE

WHEN Jenessa arrived back at the campsite that night it was dark and Finn had already gone to bed. She pulled her sleeping-bag outside, knowing she couldn't possibly share the tent with him, and lay there listening to the raindrops patter on the tarp. To her surprise she did fall asleep, although it was a sleep haunted by dreams whose details she couldn't remember the next morning but whose mood of foreboding rested heavily on her.

It was still raining, a steady drizzle from a dull grey sky. Breaking camp was down to a routine by now, which meant that she and Finn didn't have to talk to each other. She took the bow of the canoe and set a hard pace up the lake.

There were two portages, the first short but with a steep climb, the second winding through a bog where the mosquitoes were not noticeably discouraged by the rain. Jenessa had been tired before she started out. The mud sucked at her boots, making every step twice as hard, and the thwart of the canoe dug into the back of her neck, but not for anything was she going to suggest a rest. She trudged on in a fog of misery, only wanting the day to be done.

The lake that was their final destination was edged by birch meadows and low hills; there was an island in the center of the lake with granite cliffs at one end. George Hilchey had built his palatial summer house on those cliffs in such a way that its windows looked out over the vast sweep of land that had been his. Jenessa had been there only once—the visit where her father had first seen the old French maps. As the island came in sight and she saw the blank windows of the house high on the cliffs, she wished passionately that she had never set eyes on the man whose grandfather had regarded this as his kingdom.

She said, 'The dock should be behind that pointed rock.'

Finn had become a more than adequate canoeist in the last ten days. He steered toward the rotting timbers of the dock, whose uprights protruded from the water like broken teeth. Jenessa climbed out, lashing the bow to the only post that had been creosoted. Finn moved forward in the canoe and stepped on to the shore.

The rain had gentled to a fine mist. The trees stood as silent as sentinels, a thickly clustered barrier to whatever secrets the island held. The place had, Jenessa thought with a chill along her spine, that indefinable air of desolation of somewhere once inhabited and now deserted. Finn said coldly, 'I don't want you around while I'm checking out the house.'

'Fine by me,' she said.

The boughs of a venerable spruce sprang back into place after he pushed his way past them and vanished from sight. Jenessa sat down hard on the nearest rock. She was still being paid one hundred dollars a day. She should find a camping spot and start a meal; that was what she was being paid for. She lacked the energy or the desire to do either one.

Eventually she got up and made a quick reconnoiter of her surroundings. The island was not that large. She found a level area near the helicopter pad, which was now overgrown with shrubs, made several trips with all their gear, put up the tarp and made a pit for a fire. Then she took the axe and went in search of wood.

A dead maple caught her eye. Its bark was worn away, it's sharply angled lower limbs bare of smaller branches. Using her axe, she chopped at the trunk and within minutes it thudded to the ground. To her surprise a sharp clatter, as though a metal mug had struck a rock, came from between two of the branches. Curious, Jenessa bent to look.

A rectangular flat tin, which looked as though it had been wedged in the V between the branches, had fallen from its niche, hitting a chunk of granite as it landed. It was rusty, so rusty that she couldn't open it. It had been a tobacco tin, she decided. It felt too heavy to be empty.

Maybe Finn as a boy had stashed it in the maple tree, and then forgotten about it.

With a shrug she put it in one of the lower pockets on her bush pants, closing the Velcro so she wouldn't lose it. Then she took her saw and started removing the limbs one by one, a task that was so soothing in its repetitiveness that the tin slipped from her mind. After she'd carried the wood back to the fire pit, she split some for kindling, and with birch bark and small twigs started the fire. The tiny flames that clutched at the bark were oddly comforting.

She opened the Duluth packs, deciding on curried chicken and rice for dinner, and went down to the lake for water. She needed a cup of hot tea. What she really needed was at least three shots of whiskey—straight up, she amended with the first touch of humor since yesterday evening.

While the meal was cooking Jenessa put up the tent and spread some heavy plastic under the tarp for her sleeping-bag. She didn't care if there was a hurricane; she wasn't going to sleep within twenty feet of Finn Marston ever again. She fought down the desolation that that prospect caused her.

Cooking was also a soothing activity. But when everything was ready, there was no sign of Finn. He'd told her to stay away from the house; her mouth set mutinously, she started off through the trees toward the granite cliffs.

The house was made of Scandinavian cedar with a slate roof and two huge granite chimneys. From local rumor Jenessa knew George Hilchey had closed it up after his daughter's suicide; despite that, it looked solid enough to stand empty for a very long time. It was impossible for her not to contrast its imposing bulk and tall windows with the charred ruins of her father's log cabin. Yet somehow she could conjure up no rage today, no energizing surge of hatred. George Hilchey was dead now, as was his daughter and her own father. What use was hatred?

She couldn't hate the old man any more than she could bring herself to hate Finn, she thought with uncomfortable honesty. It would be better if she hated Finn. It would make more sense. How could she still love a man who had such a distorted view of the kind of woman she was?

The main door of the house opened on to a wide deck, and stood ajar. She shouted Finn's name as loudly as she could. Nothing. She climbed the quarried-stone steps to the deck and yelled his name again. Deep inside the house a door slammed. 'Finn!' she cried, and heard heavy footsteps coming down a wooden staircase two steps at a time.

Finn shoved the door wide open. His hands were filthy and there were streaks of grime on his jeans and shirt. He looked like a man driven, she thought, and wondered what he had been doing. He also looked as if he was in a towering rage. Rubbing his palms down the hips of his jeans, he snarled, 'What are you doing here?'

In a glorious flood of adrenalin that swept aside caution and restraint, Jenessa lost her temper. 'Don't you dare speak to me like that!'

'I told you to stay away!'

'Dinner's ready,' she said tautly. 'That's what I'm doing here.'

'I'll be another hour. Eat without me. And don't come back here looking for me, do you hear?'

'Do you know what?' she seethed. 'I rue the day I ever drove to the Gander airport to meet you. I've met more than my share of rude and ignorant men in my day, but you take the cake—it's a toss-up who's worse, you or your grandfather. I really don't give a damn if you *ever* come for dinner.'

Standing as she was on the deck against a blurred backdrop of silver water and hills that faded into the mist, she blazed with energy. Her eyes sparkled like emeralds; her lips were parted, her cheeks flushed, her hair tousled into damp curls. Finn took one step toward her, then jammed his hands in his pockets. 'I've never stolen anything in my life, so don't you compare me with my grandfather. And I'm not a born manipulator the way my mother was. Like you——'

Too angry to watch her words, Jenessa interrupted, 'I'm *not* like your mother. If I had a young son I wouldn't commit suicide—that's an awful thing to...'

Her voice died away. The anger had drained from Finn's body, leaving his face wrenched by far more complex emotions as he sagged against the doorframe. In true compunction she cried, 'Finn, I'm sorry; I didn't mean to——'

In a dead voice he said, 'Just go away and leave me alone, will you? I'll be back before dark.'

She turned and stumbled down the steps. When she reached the edge of the trees and looked back, the tall windows, as blank as the eyes of the dead, were all that she could see. Finn was gone, swallowed up by the house as if he didn't exist.

Although she had no appetite, Jenessa forced herself to eat. She then sat idly by the fire, feeding it damp wood that it devoured with tiny hisses of steam. Because the sky was overcast, night came early, blanketing the trees softly and imperceptibly in darkness. She made fresh tea, straining her ears for the sound of Finn's approach, and was finally rewarded when he stumbled into the clearing where the orange blaze of the fire held the darkness at bay.

He looked so exhausted, dirty and discouraged that Jenessa knew he was at the end of his tether. She said quietly, 'Sit down, Finn.' She poured warm water into a bowl so that he could wash and gave him the soap and a towel, watching as he sluiced his face and scrubbed at his grimy hands. Then she served his food, passing him his plate and pouring him a mug of tea.

He said drily, 'Heaping coals of fire, Jenessa?'

'That isn't my intent.'

Shooting her a quick look, he said, 'Thanks, it looks good.' He ate ravenously and gulped down his tea. Then, rubbing at his forehead with the back of his hand, he looked around him as though he wasn't quite sure where he was. His eyes lit on the tent, then on the plastic where she had put her sleeping-pad. He flinched as though he had been struck.

It was a strange moment for Jenessa to remember a puppy Ryan had brought home years ago; it had been mistreated, and the slightest movement in its direction had made it quiver as though it were about to be kicked. She thought quite clearly, I don't know what happened to Finn up there in the house. I do know he can't take any more.

She opened her mouth with no idea of what she was going to say. But before she could speak Finn said abruptly, 'I want out of here.'

He was telling her nothing she didn't already know. She glanced at her watch. 'It's pretty late. If we get up at dawn, we can leave here in less than——'

'I can't stay here. On this island.'

She frowned. 'You mean you want to camp somewhere else?'

As if she were being particularly slow-witted he said sarcastically, 'Yeah, that's what I mean.'

'It's pitch-dark, Finn. And I don't know the shores of this lake that well. We can't just——'

'I'm not making small talk here, I mean it—I'm not going to spend the night on this island. And if I have to pull rank, I will. It's an order, Jenessa. We're leaving here as soon as we clean up.'

She could have argued because, as the guide, she had the final say. But there were deep lines of strain around Finn's mouth and he had just spent the better part of three hours in the house where his mother had killed herself. Again she remembered the mongrel pup. 'I suppose we could cut across the lake and keep to the shore until we get to the birch meadows,' she said. 'We should be able to find somewhere there to camp.'

Easy enough to say, not as easy in practise. Because the clouds had masked the moon and stars, the darkness was thick, without relief. Jenessa sat in the bow of the canoe with a flashlight, warning Finn of rocks and dead-heads as they skirted the shoreline. The lake gleamed black; the soft gurgles of Finn's paddle sounded sinister and the overhanging boughs of the trees were like arms reaching out for them as they passed.

On the side of the hill a thin scream pierced the night as an owl pounced on its prey. The beat of the bird's wings whipped through the trees. Jenessa shivered, clutching the flashlight. Life and death were integral to nature, she had always known that, but all of a sudden she longed to be curled up in the warmth of her sleeping-bag with this interminable day put to rest.

Although their progress was slow and it was a fair-sized lake, eventually the pale trunks of the birches beckoned to them from the slopes. Reeds dragged against the sides of the canoe, then the bow bumped into the bank. Jenessa got out, swinging the light in a wide arc. The slope was steeper than she had thought. The only ground anywhere near level was beside the lake; but there were no trees there to anchor the tarp.

'Let's get the gear unloaded and the canoe up on land—then we can figure out where we're going to camp,' she said.

Tripping over rocks and roots, sliding into mudholes between the clumps of grass, they managed to dump their gear and up-end the canoe. Then Jenessa took off up the slope, searching for the small area of level ground that the tent required. The hillside was uneven and dotted with boulders; from below her, Finn, who had taken out his own flashlight, called, 'It's flat enough down here.'

She tramped down to meet him. 'There's no place for the tarp,' she said.

'It's only a light mist—does it matter?'

'If I'm going to sleep outdoors, it matters.'

His eyes like black pits, Finn said, biting off his words, 'You don't have to worry about sharing the tent with me—I won't lay a finger on you.'

If this was how love felt, why did all the magazines praise it to the skies as though it were the most desirable state a woman could achieve? 'Let's get the tent up,' Jenessa said in a dead voice.

Fifteen minutes later she was curled up in her sleeping-bag, where she had longed to be. Finn was undressing beside her; every nerve in her body cried out for him. He thinks you're a greedy little liar, she told herself fiercely, lying wide-eyed in the dark. How can you desire a man who thinks so little of you?

He slid into his own sleeping-bag; he didn't say good-night. She lay rigidly on her back, willing herself to relax, praying for sleep. But the more she wished for it, the more it eluded her. Too much had happened in the last two days... The images flashed through her tired brain, one after another, from the blackened ruins of the house where she had grown up to the defeated slump in Finn's shoulders when he had come back from his grandfather's house.

She must have fallen asleep, because suddenly she was sitting bolt upright and it was daylight and Finn was dragging his pack across the floor of the tent. She gaped at him, her thin T-shirt clinging to her breasts, her lips soft with sleep. He said curtly, 'Sorry—I didn't mean to wake you.'

Her tongue felt thick. 'What's the time?'

'Eight-thirty.'

She groaned. 'We should have been on our way an hour ago.'

'We've got some granola bars and oranges—why don't we skip breakfast and get moving?'

He was pulling on his shirt, the muscles rippling over his ribs. She averted her eyes. If the way she felt right now was anything to go by, the sooner they got back to Mac's the better. 'Okay,' she said, trying to sound practical and in control. 'There's some whitewater today...nothing too difficult but I think I should be in the stern.'

If they took advantage of the current of the river and if the weather held, they could reach the lodge in four days, Jenessa thought, bundling her bush pants into her pack and changing into lighter nylon trousers that dried more quickly. She couldn't think beyond that. The prospect of leaving Finn at the airport was more than she could imagine.

At three that afternoon she made a quick decision that they should push on, past the campsite she had tentatively selected. The breeze was with them and the rain was holding off. Besides, Finn was more than just coping with the river runs—he was actively challenged by them, obeying her shouted commands with instinctive skill and obviously understanding their logic. So it was late when she steered toward a small peninsula on a lake cupped by gently rising hills.

As they hauled the gear up and beached the canoe, she realized how tired she was. Surely she'd sleep better tonight; she had to; she couldn't go on like this. Leaving Finn to clear away some shrubs and pitch the tent, she went to get wood.

It wasn't the miles she had put on her paddle that had so exhausted her; that wasn't the problem, she decided as she picked up curls of birch bark from round the trees, her eyes constantly on the look-out for a dead tree she could chop down. The problem was Finn. Because she was sitting in the stern of the canoe, all day she had had to watch his big body moving with lean economy, the strong thrust of his arms, the twist of his torso as he fought the river currents. She wanted him physically, there was no question of that—knowledge that along with the dull ache in her belly made her feel somehow diminished. But at a much deeper level she yearned for him to see her as she was, not as he thought she was.

Impossible. Because ever since she had met him she had never been anything but herself, and that hadn't been enough.

She heaped some fallen branches with the birch bark as she sighted a couple of dead spruce. Spruce wasn't the best wood to burn, but it would have to do.

Finn despised her. Thought she had cheated him from the very day she had met him. Her eyes filming with tears, she swung the axe against the base of the trunk. Chips flew out and the tree sagged to the ground. She cut down the second spruce, lopping off the lower branches, wishing she could come up with even one strategy that might cut through the impasse in which they were trapped.

The axe struck a knot, glanced off it and bit into the soft flesh at the base of her thumb. In startled disbelief she saw drops of blood well from the cut and drip down her wrist.

She dropped the axe and fumbled for a tissue in her pocket, and as she pressed it to the cut felt the first bite of pain. The tissue stained red instantly. Automatically noticing where she had left the fallen spruce, she hurried through the trees to the campsite.

The tent was up, there were two pots of water sitting on the ground, and Finn was hunkered down constructing a fire pit, his back to her. She said, 'Could you get the first-aid kit, Finn? I've cut myself.'

He whipped around and stood up in one smooth motion, his eyes flying to the scarlet tissue pressed to her thumb. Without a wasted movement he loped to her backpack, undid the bottom compartment and pulled out a plastic box. After washing his hands in the nearest pot of water, he unwrapped a big gauze pad. 'Move your fingers,' he said.

As she obeyed, he flicked the blood-soaked tissue off and pressed the gauze against the long gash in her flesh. 'Did you do that with the axe?' he demanded, and without waiting for an answer added. 'What in hell's teeth were you thinking of?'

'You,' she said.

His dark blue eyes were turbulent with emotions she couldn't possibly have labeled. 'Are you saying your stupidity was my fault?'

The cut was throbbing and Jenessa didn't need him telling her how stupid she'd been. She already knew that. 'No,' she said baldly, and prayed she wouldn't humiliate herself by bursting into tears.

Finn glanced at her. She was pale, her jaw rigid against the pain; the falling light shadowed her eyes. He muttered, 'I shouldn't have said that... I'm sorry.'

It was the first intimation in what seemed like a very long time of the man who had made love to her with such bliss. I won't cry, I won't, she thought, and saw a tear plop on to the back of his hand.

'Jenessa—don't,' he said hoarsely.

'It hurts, that's all.'

Easing the pad away, he said, 'It's a clean cut, and not as deep as I first thought.' He gave her a wintry smile. 'I've had first-aid training but I've never had to stitch anyone up—be glad you're not the first one. Here, sit down on this rock and keep the pressure on it. Where's the tree that caused the damage?'

She gave him directions, glad enough to sink down on the rock because her knees were trembling. She was lucky. It could have been a lot worse. A new rule to add to the guide handbook, she thought ruefully: never travel with an estranged lover.

With an efficiency that didn't surprise her in the least, Finn came back with the wood, started a fire and put water on to boil. He then put antibiotic cream on the cut and bound up her hand. After he had given her a mug of herbal tea, he started supper.

Jenessa sipped the mint tea. It was comforting, as was the heat of the flames. But after that single outburst Finn had treated her as impersonally as a chance-met stranger, and neither tea nor fire could melt the cold lump lodged somewhere in the vicinity of her heart.

She ate everything on her plate and five minutes afterwards would have had difficulty relating what she had swallowed. Finn said with characteristic abruptness, 'Is your hand hurting?'

Too stubborn to lie, she said, 'Yes.'

'I'll clean up—you go to bed.'

Tears were painfully close to the surface again. I'm cracking up, Jenessa thought wildly, and wondered what had happened to the competent, detached woman she had always prided herself on being. 'Goodnight,' she mumbled, and pushed herself up from the rock.

'Will you need any help with your clothes?'

She winced. 'No, thanks.'

His mouth tightened. 'I hope you'll sleep well,' he said stiffly, and thrust another log into the fire. The flames danced over his face, so familiar to her, so closed against her. Jenessa hurried to the tent and crawled inside.

It was a relief to be alone. She struggled out of her outer garments and eased herself into her sleeping-bag, cupped her sore hand to her breast and closed her eyes. Like a dead weight sleep fell on her, smothering her in its thick folds.

CHAPTER THIRTEEN

JENESSA woke as the first light of day illuminated the interior of the tent. When she opened her eyes, she was looking straight at Finn, his irises so dark a blue as to be unreadable. Wondering if she was dreaming, she reached up to rub her face, felt the clench of pain in her palm and knew she was indeed awake.

In the night she had turned over to face his side of the tent. He was lying on his back, half propped against his pack, his hands linked behind his head. He had been watching her while she slept, she realized in a flash of fury. He despised her, yet he chose to stare at her when she was at her most vulnerable.

'How's your hand?' he asked in a voice as unreadable as his face.

She flexed her palm. 'Feels okay. Let's get moving.'

'You don't think we should take a day off? Give the cut a chance to close over?'

'No,' she said in a brittle voice, 'I don't. I'm as anxious to get to Mac's as you are, Finn.'

'Although scarcely for the same reasons,' he sneered.

Her brain felt heavy, and sleep seemed to have done nothing to remove a bone-deep exhaustion. 'For exactly the same reasons—I want this charade over, too.'

She could have said, I can't wait to see the last of you. But it would have been utterly untrue.

'Tell me something,' he said with deadly quietness. 'Was the lovemaking a charade for you, Jenessa?'

Her pride demanded that she lie. It was pride that had enabled her to survive the terrors of the schoolyard all those years ago; she knew its value only too well. But she wasn't fourteen any more. She was twenty-five years old, face to face with the one man who had called her to full womanhood. The cost of that emergence had been high. But, no matter what happened, having met Finn she would never see the world in the same way again. Jenessa pushed herself up on her elbow, feeling at a disadvantage lying on her side, and said, 'Not for me, it wasn't a charade. Was it for you?'

He twisted to face her, the pale light falling softly on the hollows and planes of his chest. 'Do you know how I've felt ever since I met you?' he said violently. 'As though I've been dropped in the wilderness without a compass or a map, no bearings at all... and left to find my way out as best I can.'

Her heart beating as rapidly as if she'd been running rather than sleeping, Jenessa said steadily, 'When you're lost in the woods, you look for the path of the sun. You look for the mosses on the south flanks of the trees... there are always signs.'

'And what if you don't trust those signs—if nothing in your life has given you cause to trust them?'

'If you're truly lost, you have to trust them. They're all you've got.'

'You make it sound so easy—too easy,' he said with the same repressed violence. 'And no, Jenessa, it wasn't a charade for me either.'

For a moment between them hung all the memories of their shared passion. Unconsciously Jenessa made a small pleading gesture with her bandaged hand. Finn said levelly, 'Which would hurt your hand less—packing up or cooking breakfast?'

He had retreated again. 'Breakfast,' she said.

As she made buckwheat pancakes and coffee, her cut bothered her more than she would have admitted. The meal over, she dried the dishes that Finn washed, then he said, 'I'll rebandage your hand.'

The wound looked clean, although as Finn gently pressed the surrounding skin she couldn't help flinching. He said, 'I'll paddle in the stern today; that'll make it easier for you.'

'You can't—we've got a long river run.'

'One thing I sure trust is your stubbornness!'

In Jenessa's breast all the tensions of the last three days coalesced into rage. 'Yes, my hand's sore and yes, if things were different there's nothing I'd like better than to spend a day around here,' she exploded. 'But they aren't different—according to you I manipulated you from the start to get my hands on your grandfather's land. You can do what you like with the land, Finn Marston—make an amusement park out of it, cut down every tree and pave it from end to end—I really don't care. Just let's get out of here!'

'It can't be too soon for me,' he snarled, taped the bandage in place and dropped her hand as though it were poison.

Within ten minutes they were on their way. The freshening breeze was a headwind. Jenessa paddled hard all morning and by the time they stopped for a snack lunch had a headache that was pounding in turn with the throbbing in her palm. They had negotiated three sets of riffles that morning; in the afternoon the river deepened, the current moving with deceptive placidity between banks of tumbled granite. Coming round a bend they surprised two caribou in midstream; Jenessa steered for an eddy, and she and Finn watched as the animals splashed toward a gravel beach and trotted with their high-kneed gait out of sight through the trees.

Pave the land from end to end, she had said. Who had she been kidding?

For another three miles the river continued its gradual descent. Then, as they rounded another bend, they heard the dull roar of rapids and saw a cloud of spray hanging over the dark, serrated line where the river disappeared from sight. Well upstream from it, Jenessa headed for the shore. Once they'd landed she said, 'We'll have to portage these rapids. But I think we can run the ones below them... it's a two-mile stretch.'

The portage to circumvent the rapids was steep and difficult. As she and Finn gripped the gunwales and lowered the canoe back in the water, he rapped, 'Your hand's bleeding again—it's soaked through the bandage. You'd better let me look at it.'

Her temples were being squeezed in a vise and she couldn't bear the thought of him touching her. 'I don't see why you're so worried,' she flashed. 'You hate my guts, Finn, admit it.'

Not waiting for a reply, she looped the painter round a tree and bent to pick up the nearest pack. 'Leave those, I'll get them,' Finn snapped, pulled her upright and kissed her full on the lips.

The shock ran through Jenessa's body. She remembered it all so well: the strength of his arms, the solid wall of his chest, the warmth of his mouth against hers. Fighting the memories, she thrust herself backward and gasped, 'Don't you ever dare do that to me again!'

'At least that was real.'

She had no answer for him, wasn't even sure she knew any more what was real and what was—to use her own word—charade. She stood by mutely as Finn reloaded the canoe, waited while he settled himself in the bow, then climbed in the stern and pushed off, already busying her mind with the course she'd steer.

Everything went smoothly for the first mile and a half. Finn had a natural grasp of what to do; they were,

Jenessa thought unhappily, paddling very much as a team. They eddied out so that she could check the last run of the rapids, where the water slid as sleek as an otter's back between the boulders. Then they steered back into the current.

She backpaddled and braced until the channel opened in front of her. In a hard power stroke she dug her paddle into the water. But the blade struck a rock hidden below the surface; the shock raced through the shaft and along her arm to her injured palm, blossoming into a pain so sudden and so fierce that the paddle was wrenched from her grasp. She grabbed for it and overbalanced, the river rushing up to meet her. Instinctively she kicked herself free of the canoe. Then water filled her ears and her nose and her mouth; she was drowning in a sea of bubbles. A rock struck her hip with bruising force.

Again Jenessa instinctively did the right thing. Feet first with the current—a lesson her father and Ryan had drummed into her ever since she had been old enough to be in a canoe. She surfaced, gulped for air, and saw blue sky and white clouds swing overhead. Too late, she also saw that she was being driven straight toward a rough-edged chunk of granite as big as a boatshed. She lunged sideways in a desperate effort to avoid it, felt the rock hit her foot and scrape her flesh from ankle to knee, and was thrust into the swirling waters of the eddy that rippled toward the riverbank.

Choking, she surfaced again, fighting for air. The eddy was deep, overhung by an ancient maple tree whose topmost leaves were already stained scarlet. She seized one of the lower branches and looked back over her shoulder.

Finn had turned in his seat so that in effect he was now paddling from the stern. With a series of powerful draws he was pulling the canoe into the eddy. He was safe, she thought dazedly, with a relief so strong she almost forgot to tread water. From the instant she had tipped out of the canoe she had been terrified that Finn might have capsized and drowned.

He drove the canoe toward her, stopped it in a swirl of spray and said jaggedly, 'Jenessa—are you all right?'

She felt bruised and cold and humiliated. 'Yes,' she said.

'You scared me out of ten years' growth.' He looked around. 'Grab the gunwale. I'll head for the bank.'

Meekly she did as she was told. He landed the canoe, tied the painter around the maple tree and knelt to help her up. Her leg didn't want to support her...wouldn't support her. Her eyes widened. 'I—I can't stand up,' she stuttered.

Finn grasped her under the armpits and, with a strength that afterwards she would marvel at, heaved her up over the rocks and away from the water. After he had put her down on a carpet of springy needles under a white pine, he crouched beside her. Her nylon trousers had ripped as easily if they were made of paper. Blood and river water were streaming pink down her shin. Jenessa said in dismay, 'I'm a disaster area—how could I have been so stupid?'

'Stay put,' Finn ordered, 'while I get the first-aid kit.'

Between one moment and the next as she sat alone in the little clearing Jenessa became aware of pain. It started innocently enough with a sharp twinge as she shifted her knee; her cut hand was throbbing again, she realized, and she had ruined a pair of perfectly good nylon pants. The twinge didn't go away; rather, it gradually spread and intensified, until her whole leg from knee to ankle was burning as if it were on fire.

Finn dropped to his knees beside her. He eased the tarp under her so that she wasn't sitting on the damp ground, took one look at her white face and said, 'You've got to get out of those wet clothes.' He pulled a towel and some dry garments from her pack, removed her life-jacket and swiftly hauled her drenched sweater over her head. Her skin was covered in goose-bumps, her nipples tight. Jenessa took the towel from him, hating her nakedness, wanting only to hide it from him, and, because she knew him so well, saw his instant reading of her motives. His eyes darkened. With scant ceremony he dragged a dry sweater over her head and wrapped a jacket round her shoulders.

'You'll have to cut my trousers off,' she said faintly. 'Be careful—it hurts.'

Finn was very gentle, for which she was grateful. When her trousers were lying in a sodden heap on the tarp, he said, 'You're not bleeding that much—but there are little flakes of mica from the granite caught in the scrape. I'm going to boil some water, and then I'll have to clean it as best I can.'

She nodded, knowing that she would have done exactly what he was suggesting. She could hear herself breathing in shallow gasps, and she felt very cold; as if he had read her mind, Finn took off his fleece shirt and covered her thighs, then scrambled back down the bank and got the rest of the packs, which he stacked behind her as a windbreak. 'It'll take me a few minutes to get wood,' he said, 'Hang in there, Jenessa.'

His shirt carried the warmth and scent of his body; she rested her forehead on it, biting her lip against the pain. When Finn came back to the clearing with an armload of wood, her shoulders were rigid with the effort not to weep. He rummaged in the first-aid kit, found a small bottle of pain-killers, and made her take one. 'Yell or scream if it'll make you feel better,' he said grimly.

'You don't have to be a stoic.' Then he built a fire and put some water on to boil.

All this took time. The codeine made Jenessa feel dizzy and sick; she drifted into a daze where the leaping flames and the burning in her leg were one and the same. While he waited for the water to boil and then to cool, Finn set up the tent to one side of the clearing and scouted for more wood. Eventually, after he had scrubbed his hands, he said, 'Why don't you take another pill, Jenessa? This is going to hurt.'

'They make me feel worse,' she muttered. 'I'll be okay.'

Although Finn was exquisitely careful, he did hurt her. She buried her face in her arms and dug her teeth into her wrist, not quite able to suppress tiny, animal-like sounds of pain as he cleaned the dirt from the wound. Finally she felt him apply pads coated with a cool antibiotic cream, and tape them in place. In a voice she hadn't heard him use before he said, 'It's done.'

When she looked up his eyes fell on her wrist, where the marks of her teeth had indented the skin. 'For God's sake, sweetheart,' he muttered.

He was white about the mouth, beads of sweat trickling down his forehead. 'No, I'm not,' Jenessa said, her voice a thin thread. 'Your sweetheart, I mean. You hate me.'

Finn swiped at his forehead; his fingers were not quite steady. 'The last ten minutes did away with any pretensions I might have had toward hating you—believe me.'

'You might not hate me—but you still don't trust me.'

He looked straight at her. 'If I don't trust you, then I can't trust the ground I'm kneeling on.'

The intensity of his gaze disturbed her deeply. Smoothing the tarp with her fingers, she burst out, 'I could have drowned both of us back there—I'd never have forgiven myself if anything had happened to you, Finn.'

'You're changing the subject.'

Her nostrils flared. 'I don't have the energy for another fight.'

He said with some of his old impatience, 'Okay—so you made a mistake out there in the river. You're human, not perfect, Jenessa, and we all make mistakes. I made one the day I hurt my ribs at the blowout. And if anyone's responsible for what happened today, I am—I know what I've put you through the last few days. I may be out of touch with my feelings, but I'm not totally blind.'

Jenessa's heart was beating in thick, heavy strokes. She mumbled, 'You should get out of your wet clothes.'

'You don't have a clue what I'm trying to tell you, do you?' As Finn pushed her hair back from her forehead, there was still the lightest of tremors in his fingers. 'I've been kidding myself for days, Jenessa. I don't hate you. I love you.'

Jenessa blinked, trying to push away the mists of pain and codeine. 'I've knocked myself out and I'm dreaming,' she quavered. 'Or else I've died and gone to heaven.'

She wasn't even sure he'd heard her. 'You've got to be real. Or nothing's real.'

With considerable effort Jenessa held on to her train of thought. 'Did you say you loved me, Finn? Or am I delirious?'

'That's what I said.'

She dredged up a vestige of her normal energy. 'You don't look very happy about it.'

'After the way I've treated you? No wonder you can't bear for me to kiss you.'

Finn loved her . . . *loved* her. Feeling as though she was floating about three inches above the ground, Jenessa announced, 'For an intelligent man, you can be pretty stupid sometimes. I love you too.'

'I know I can't expect—*what*?'

She said it a second time, more loudly. 'I love you—that's what I said.'

In the novel that Ruth had loaned her, Finn would now have enfolded her in his arms and carried her to the nearest satin-sheeted bed. Instead he said blankly, 'Why?'

The codeine, combined with requited love, appeared to have removed any brakes on Jenessa's tongue. 'That's a question I've asked myself quite often in the last few days.' She scowled in thought. 'Because you're you, I suppose. I'd be the first to admit my experience is somewhat limited, but it seems to me that you learn quite a lot about a man when you make love with him. I guess I really liked what I learned about you, Finn. I know I liked the things you did to me.' Her scowl deepened. 'I hated it when you said lovemaking had nothing to do with love. And I hated it even worse when you accused me of leading you on to get my rapacious little hands on your inheritance.'

'I——'

'Why did you do that, Finn? Why did you think the absolute worst of me?'

She eased her back against the nearest pack, grimacing as she jarred her leg, knowing the question itself and its answer were all-important. Finn hesitated. 'I've never talked to anyone about this,' he said. 'I never let anyone close enough so that I'd have to.'

'You've got to now. Because you can't say you love me and then think the worst of me whenever things go wrong.'

As though a dam had opened so that all the water gushed out, Finn said, 'It goes back a long time—to the way I was brought up. My mother never wanted me or loved me from the day I was born, and I never knew why. As a little boy I tried everything I could think of to make her love me. As an adolescent I rebelled in classic and I'm sure quite unbearable fashion, and as soon as I turned sixteen I left home and struck out on my own. Four months after I left, she committed suicide—in the summer house——'

He broke off, staring into the dancing flames. Jenessa sat very still, terrified of breaking into his train of thought. 'I've carried the guilt for her death with me ever since,' Finn said in a low voice. 'Maybe she did love me after all, and just couldn't express it... and when I left she fell apart. Now that I look back as an adult, I think she probably suffered from depression most of her life. Maybe my leaving was what tipped her over the edge.'

He stirred the coals with a stick, watching them pulse and glow. 'Whatever the reason, I've kept my distance from women all my life. Oh, I've had the occasional affair over the years, as long as the woman was no more interested in commitment than I was. But until I met you I never figured I'd fall in love. Didn't think I knew how. Which is no doubt why I've been fighting it—and you—ever since we met... You scared me out of my wits.' He looked straight at her. 'And if some of my methods were less than honorable, that's a measure both of my fear and the depth of my love.'

As if it was the most natural thing in the world Jenessa sagged against his shoulder and felt his arms go round her. 'I'm sorry your mother died like that,' she whispered. 'But it can't have been your fault, Finn.'

'I'll never know that. But I do know something—know it in my blood and my bones. I love you. It wasn't until I had to hurt you a few minutes ago that I realized just how much...and what a fool I'd been to try and run away from you.'

Jenessa gave a sigh of happiness. 'I never thought I'd hear you say those words.'

Very gently Finn lifted her face from his shoulder and kissed her, a kiss unlike any other he had ever given her because it breathed of the way he felt. Although her green eyes were shining, Jenessa was still very pale. 'How are you feeling?' he said.

'Awful,' she replied with a dazzling smile. 'And awfully happy.'

'Bed for you,' Finn said. 'Then I'll make you something to eat.' With a grin that touched her heart he added, 'One sleeping-bag, so I can hold on to you all night.'

Her own smile was wobbly. 'In Ruth's book we'd now make mad passionate love the whole night through.'

Finn said very quietly, 'We've got the rest of our lives for that, Jenessa.'

Her eyes filled with easy tears. 'Do you really mean that?'

'I want to marry you. If you'll have me.'

'Oh, yes,' said Jenessa, and planted a kiss somewhere in the vicinity of his mouth.

When Jenessa woke up, it was still dark and she was curled into Finn's chest. Finn loves me, she thought, feeling as though the sun had suddenly risen in the confines of the tent and she was basking in its heat. Finn wants to marry me. This is what felicity is like...I never knew.

At a more mundane level, her leg hurt. Feeling his breath stir her hair, she snuggled a little closer. Finn and

I are going to get married... If someone had told me yesterday morning that by evening he'd have proposed to me, I'd have told them they were crazy.

Aren't you the one who's crazy? a little voice whispered in her brain. If you marry Finn, you'll have to leave Newfoundland. Leave the job you love and the countryside that's been your lifeblood ever since you were born. And Finn will be traveling all over the world, wherever his job takes him...how will you like that, Jenessa? It's a very dangerous job, too. Much more dangerous than yours.

She lay still, hating the insidious little voice, yet unable to discount what it had said. She hadn't even considered the practical aspects of marriage last night; she had been too happy. She didn't want to consider them now. Yet there they were, inescapable.

'What's wrong, Jenessa?' Finn said softly.

She gave a guilty start. 'I thought you were asleep.'

'Is your leg hurting?'

'Will I have to leave Newfoundland?' she blurted. 'And my job? I don't want to do that, Finn.'

He chuckled. 'I wondered when you'd get around to that. After you went to sleep last night, I started figuring out the logistics of how we're actually going to manage to live together. Because I want you in my bed as many nights of the week as possible. What with computers and fax machines my office can be anywhere in the world, as long as I'm near an airport. How about Halifax or St John's in the winters and Gander in summer? That way you can keep on guiding for as long as you want to. I've decided I'm going to take on more of an administrative role in my company, too, which will ease the amount of traveling I do.'

'Don't you need the danger?' Jenessa said doubtfully.

'I don't think I will nearly as much as I used to. Some of it was part of running away—you were right about that.'

Humbled, she added, 'You sat and worked all that out last night?'

This time Finn laughed outright. 'Wonderful how sublimated sex clarifies the brain.'

She nuzzled his chest. 'I promise it won't have to be sublimated for long.'

'Quit distracting me, woman,' he growled, 'because I haven't finished—I'm going to deed my grandfather's land to you. As a wedding present.'

She pushed back so that she could look into his eyes. 'You *do* trust me,' she said shakily. 'That's what that means... that you really do trust me.'

'Love's all or nothing, isn't it? I've learned that much since last night. Love, trust, respect—they all go together.'

'I'll turn the land into a wildlife sanctuary, if that's okay with you.'

'Never did like the idea of Mac blasting away at the caribou... How's your leg?'

'Sore—and nature's calling,' she admitted.

He rummaged in her pack, tossing her a pair of bush pants. As she eased them over her bandaged leg, something hard bumped her knee. Puzzled, she felt in the pocket and retrieved a small, rusty tin. 'Oh, I remember this,' she said casually. 'It fell out of the maple tree I cut down by your grandfather's lodge—I meant to ask you if it was yours.'

Finn was staring at the tin as though it might bite him. 'The old maple with the forked branches... of course,' he whispered. 'Why didn't I think of that?'

Jenessa handed it to him, then, bodily needs taking precedence over curiosity—for the tin had clearly brought back memories of his boyhood—she pushed her feet into her sneakers and very carefully crawled out of the tent.

The sky was the pale cream of dawn, and a spider had constructed a web of astounding, dew-sprinkled beauty between two pine branches. The river murmured between the trees. Finn and I love each other, Jenessa thought with an uprush of joy, feeling as though the morning had been created afresh just for her.

In a burr of wings a chickadee flew into the tree. As the web rocked gently, the dew caught the first rays of the sun, splintering into all the hues of the rainbow. The pine needles had never looked so green or the boughs so graceful; the air smelled of fallen needles and resin and the dank, rich scent of the riverbank.

A second chickadee joined the first. Chittering back and forth, they flitted among the branches. Now that Finn and I are together, I'm more truly a part of this world that I love, Jenessa thought slowly. I've found my mate, the man who completes me. And one day I hope I'll give birth to his child, as is the way of nature.

Joy was lingering in her face when she edged back into the tent a few minutes later. But the sight of Finn's face drove it away. 'What's wrong?' she said sharply.

He looked stunned, almost as though someone had just hit him over the head. 'The tin,' he croaked. 'It had a letter in it from my mother. She used to do oil paintings while she was at the summer house, and there was one on her bedroom wall of that maple tree—but I never made the connection and thought to look there.'

'Look for what?' Jenessa asked in confusion.

'That was why I wanted to go to the summer house,' he said impatiently. 'To see if she'd left any kind of a message for me, explaining why she never loved me, why she killed herself. I'd already gone through all my grandfather's papers and found nothing. So the house was my last hope. And, of course, I found nothing there either, even though I searched high and low.'

Feeling her way, Jenessa said, 'So that was how you got so dirty that day... and why you wanted to leave the island even though it was dark.'

He held up two sheets of notepaper, closely written in a cramped hand. 'She wrote it all down. The truth. More for her own salvation than for mine, I think... but now at least I know.'

'What does it say?'

Finn took a deep breath. 'I always knew that my grandfather was a tyrant, an oppressive, angry man. My mother—his only child—was a girl to start with, not a boy. So she was a disappointment from the beginning. But all her life she tried to please him, even to marrying the man her father chose for her. But then she disappointed him again. As the years went by she had no child, no boy to be an heir to all that my grandfather had accumulated... Do you know what he did, that wicked old man?'

Jenessa couldn't begin to imagine. Not waiting for her to answer, Finn went on, 'He sent her and my father away for a year, ostensibly on business. But he'd arranged for an adoption there—me—and when they came back he made her say I was her own son. So I was forced on her, the truth smothered for the sake of appearances and my grandfather's overweening pride. No wonder she never loved me.'

Jenessa frowned. 'Why did she go along with it?'

'She was terrified of her father. All her life. So she never dared to defy him openly. Instead she buried all her anger... the classic cause of depression.' Finn smoothed the pages of the letter with one hand and went on in a cracked voice, 'She as much as says here that her life never had any meaning. But she waited to kill herself until I was gone. She didn't do that to me while we lived under the same roof.'

'The poor woman...' Jenessa said with instinctive sympathy.

A sheen of tears in his eyes, Finn said, 'I wish she hadn't ended it. I wish she and I could have met as adults and tried to sort some of this mess out. Who knows? Maybe we could have grown to love each other.'

Jenessa rested her hand on his wrist. 'Is she the reason you didn't respect women?'

'She never stood up to my grandfather. Never fought him. Never said no. Just once in her life I wanted her to tell him off. Instead she tried to get what she wanted covertly, using deceit and subterfuge and manipulation—all the things I accused you of.' He looked up. 'From the day you and I met you sure knew how to say no. You despised me for offering you fifteen hundred dollars a week; you couldn't be bought or made to do anything you didn't want to. But when I found out about your ties to my grandfather's land, I slotted you right alongside my mother and figured you'd been deceiving me from the start.' He grimaced. 'I was wrong—couldn't have been more wrong. It sounds futile to say I'm sorry...but I am.'

'I do understand,' Jenessa said. Still troubled, she added, 'Perhaps your mother was glad when you left, Finn. Glad that you hadn't succumbed to your grandfather's way of life, but were carving out your own.'

'Yeah,' he said wryly. 'In a business that was so dangerous that I just about killed myself, a business where I didn't take a proper holiday in ten years.'

'It will be different now,' Jenessa said with deep conviction.

Finn nodded. 'Different because I've learned from you about the power of love. A lesson I needed, although I was the last one to realize that. You see, we always fought, my grandfather and I, from the day I was old enough to defy him.' He gave an unamused laugh. 'His will says it all. He left me a parcel of land he must have known I'd see as useless. He didn't leave me a cent of his money. All along, I realize now, he knew I wasn't his true grandson. I wasn't part of the bloodline, a real member of his family.'

So it wasn't only her father's life that George Hilchey had ruined, Jenessa thought, appalled. He had done the same for his own daughter; and even from the grave he hadn't forgiven his adopted, errant grandson.

'It's ironic, isn't it,' Finn said, 'that his will led me directly to you? The greatest gift I could possibly have received.'

Tears in her eyes, Jenessa murmured, 'The gift of love.'

'The only gift worth having,' said Finn.

EPILOGUE

FIVE weeks later Jenessa was hurrying down the stairs that led from her bedroom to Ryan's kitchen. She was going to be late; it had taken her longer to get ready than she'd thought. In the doorway she halted, suddenly shy. Three pairs of eyes fastened themselves on her.

'Jenessa,' Ruth breathed, 'you look terrific!'

Baby Stephen waved his arms in the air, burbled something incomprehensible and gave a big grin; his pink gums now boasted three shiny new teeth.

Ryan put his fingers in the corners of his mouth and whistled loudly and uncouthly. 'You've sure pulled out all the stops,' he said. 'Poor guy doesn't have a hope. You forgot to do up your shirt, though. And what's wrong with your skirt? Did they run out of thread when they were sewing it up?'

'Shut up, Ryan,' Ruth ordered; 'it's a very sexy skirt.'

The skirt in question was calf-length, black and slim-fitting, the front and back seams split to well above Jenessa's knees. Her teal-green silk shirt bared her throat. The long gold chain Finn had sent from Venezuela for her birthday gleamed between her breasts, while the ear-rings he had mailed from New York twinkled below her new hairdo. She was wearing polished black leather boots and sheer black hose; her injured leg had healed over. 'Do I look all right?' she said anxiously.

'Fabulous,' Ruth sighed, and for a moment sounded just like her mother. 'This is so romantic.'

Ryan picked up his brush and dipped it in the paint can. 'Not bad,' he said gruffly. 'Not as good as this bird's goin' to look when I'm done. But not bad.'

Jenessa glanced at the clock. 'I'd better go, or I'll be late.' She dropped a kiss on Stephen's soft head, hugged Ruth and ruffled Ryan's hair. 'Don't stay up for me,' she said with a touch of insouciance. 'I don't know what time I'll be home.'

'I'm not expectin' to see either one of you before breakfast,' Ryan said, painting the duck's bill dull orange.

Jenessa blushed, Ruth said, 'Off you go in case the plane's early,' and Stephen waved both his fat little arms at her.

Jenessa wasn't used to driving in elegant leather boots. But she made it to the airport without mishap and parked the van. The plane was already taxiing down the runway. She hurried inside, her heels clicking on the floor. The dour old commissionaire, whom she'd known for years, did a double take when he saw her then actually produced a smile. Among the small crowd waiting for the plane two of her friends didn't recognize her right away. Maybe Finn won't recognize me, she thought, her stomach cramping with nervousness. She should have worn her bush pants and her rubber boots.

But he still loved her. Or he had two nights ago when he'd phoned her from New York, where he was closing out one of his offices. They hadn't been able to talk for nearly two weeks while she'd been out on the barrens with the film crew; it had been the longest two weeks of her whole life.

The loudspeaker announced the arrival of the evening flight. Jenessa clutched her new leather purse to her side and wished her heart would stop trying to pummel its way out of her chest.

Through the open door from the runway strode a tall, dark-haired man in a grey business suit, carrying a leather briefcase. He looked around impatiently, an impatience she remembered all too well. Then his eyes lit on her, taking in every detail of her appearance. Rooted to the spot, Jenessa gazed back. He was a stranger, she thought in panic, this well-groomed man in his immaculate suit with its tailored shirt and silk tie. A stranger as seven weeks ago he had been a stranger.

Then Finn closed the distance between them and she saw that his irises were the same dark blue, the expression in them sending a ripple of anticipation along her spine. He put down his briefcase. 'Jenessa...I didn't think you could possibly be more beautiful than I remembered you,' he said, and bent his head to kiss her.

His lips, the clean masculine scent of his skin, the strength of his arms—they were all the same, Jenessa thought in deep relief, and kissed him back.

It was a long and thorough kiss that made nonsense of the month they had spent apart. Against her hair Finn murmured, 'Not a trace of wood smoke.'

She chuckled. 'I should hope not—I'm wearing the perfume you sent me from Texas.'

'Still love me?'

'Oh, yes.'

He kissed her again with a very satisfactory degree of passion—rather more passion than was suitable for an airport terminal. 'I love you too. I very much want to show you how much I love you. I booked a room in the best motel in town—will Ryan mind?'

'Ryan isn't expecting us until breakfast.'

'We might make it by then,' Finn said. 'Providing it's not an early breakfast.'

'I don't think it'll be too early...he has six decoys to finish tonight.'

'Good,' said Finn. 'I want you to myself for at least twelve hours.'

Fifteen hours had passed by the time Jenessa and Finn walked in the back door at Ryan's, and the six decoys were already packed in a shipping crate. But Ryan had only just put the coffee on to brew. 'Figured you wouldn't get here before eleven,' he leered. 'What's that rock on your finger, Jenny?'

It was a beautifully cut emerald in an intricate gold setting. 'My engagement ring,' Jenessa said.

''Bout time,' Ryan said. 'Already had Ruth's mum on the phone this morning wantin' to find out what's goin' on. I told her I was plannin' on walkin' you up the aisle before Christmas; that's what I told her.'

'That's too long to wait,' said Finn.

'You'll have to buy a new suit, Ryan,' Jenessa threatened. 'And have a haircut.'

Ryan gave a rude snort, put a pan of muffins in the oven and got out the coffee-mugs. 'We might as well call this lunch,' he said.

"All it takes is one letter to trigger a romance"

***Sealed with a Kiss*—don't miss this exciting new mini-series every month.**

All the stories involve a relationship which develops as a result of a letter being written—we know you'll love these new heart-warming romances.

And to make them easier to identify, all the covers in this series are a passionate pink!

Available now **Price: £1.99**

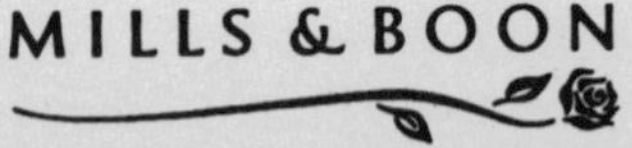

Available from W.H. Smith, John Menzies, Volume One, Forbuoys, Martins, Woolworths, Tesco, Asda, Safeway and other paperback stockists.

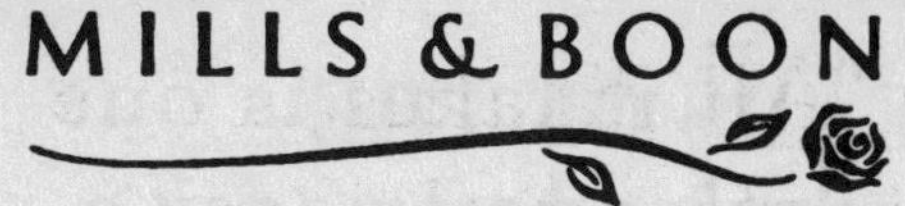

Next Month's Romances

Each month you can choose from a wide variety of romance with Mills & Boon. Below are the new titles to look out for next month.

THE LAST GRAND PASSION	Emma Darcy
THE BALLEYMORE BRIDE	Emma Goldrick
THE SISTER SWAP	Susan Napier
SLAVE TO LOVE	Michelle Reid
BOND OF HATRED	Lynne Graham
MAIL-ORDER BRIDEGROOM	Day Leclaire
LACE AND SATIN	Helen Brooks
DANGEROUS PRETENCE	Stephanie Howard
IMPERFECT STRANGER	Elizabeth Oldfield
SEASCAPE	Anne Weale
PASSIONATE INHERITANCE	Rebecca King
A LITTLE CORNER OF PARADISE	Catherine Spencer
WICKED SEDUCTION	Christine Greig
PRACTISED DECEIVER	Susanne McCarthy
RELUCTANT DESIRE	Kay Gregory
DARK TEMPTATION	Joanna Mansell

Available from WH Smith, John Menzies, Volume One, Forbuoys, Martins, Woolworths, Tesco, Asda, Safeway and other paperback stockists.

TEARS OF THE RENEGADE

Linda Howard

The world stopped for Susan Blackstone when she saw the stranger—and her heart stopped when she learned his name. He was Cord Blackstone, the black sheep of the family, and her own cousin by marriage.

Cord had come back for just one reason: revenge. But he hadn't counted on Susan any more than she had counted on him. Searing passion became the wild card in the battle for control of the family business—and it was too soon to know who had been dealt the winning card.

"You can't just read one Linda Howard!"

Catherine Coulter